EDDIE
THE DOG HOLDER

By the Same Author

ROBERT ROWS THE RIVER. 1965
  (*Weekly Reader Book Club Selection*)
EDDIE'S GREEN THUMB. 1964
  (*Weekly Reader Book Club Selection*)
HERE COMES THE BUS! 1963
SNOWBOUND WITH BETSY. 1962
ANNIE PAT AND EDDIE. 1960
EDDIE AND LOUELLA. 1959
BETSY'S WINTERHOUSE. 1958
EDDIE MAKES MUSIC. 1957
BETSY'S BUSY SUMMER. 1956
EDDIE AND HIS BIG DEALS. 1955
BETSY AND THE CIRCUS. 1954
EDDIE'S PAY DIRT. 1953
THE MIXED-UP TWINS. 1952
EDDIE AND GARDENIA. 1951
BETSY'S LITTLE STAR. 1950
EDDIE AND THE FIRE ENGINE. 1949
PENNY GOES TO CAMP. 1948
LITTLE EDDIE. 1947

Published by William Morrow & Company

PENNY AND PETER. 1946
BETSY AND THE BOYS. 1945
HERE'S A PENNY. 1944
BACK TO SCHOOL WITH BETSY. 1943
PRIMROSE DAY. 1942
BETSY AND BILLY. 1941
TWO AND TWO ARE FOUR. 1940
"B" IS FOR BETSY. 1939

Published by Harcourt, Brace & World

WEEKLY READER CHILDREN'S BOOK CLUB

presents

EDDIE
THE DOG HOLDER

written and illustrated by
CAROLYN HAYWOOD

William Morrow and Company

New York

To

Stuart Y. McDougal

who prepared for kindergarten, grammar school,

high school, and college with the Eddie books.

CONTENTS

1. Aunt Mabel's Cocker Spaniel   13

2. Eddie Goes to a Party   31

3. Painting Buster   52

4. Now It's a German Shepherd   71

5. Boodles' Birthday Present   95

6. A Yankee-Doodle Dog   112

7. Valuable Property   131

8. An Unexpected Caller   153

9. Back to School   171

EDDIE
THE DOG HOLDER

Chapter One

AUNT MABEL'S COCKER
SPANIEL

IT WAS the first day of July and school had been closed for a week. Eddie Wilson was wandering around the house trying to decide what to do with himself. Usually he had a stray animal or two to feed or wash or brush. There had been times when he had spent a whole morning pulling burrs out of a dog's coat. The Wilson household had been without an animal for a long time and Eddie felt lonely. Even old Fleetfoot the turtle hadn't been around for days.

Eddie had made several trips to the cookie jar and poured himself three glasses of milk when his mother said, "Eddie, can't you find anything to do but eat and drink?"

"I wish I had a dog or something," said Eddie. "Any kind of an animal would do. Even a skunk."

"Why don't you go over to Boodles' house and see what he's doing?" his mother suggested.

"He's gone away for the Fourth of July," Eddie replied.

"Well, Sidney is right next door," said his mother. "Why don't you go over to Sidney's?"

"Sid's little cousin Susie is there. When she's with Susie Sid gets all mushy and darlingish."

"Darlingish!" said his mother. "What do you mean?"

"Oh, you know," said Eddie. "It's 'Now darling' this and 'Now darling' that. Oh, it's awful. Sid's just a mess when she gets darlingish. Most of the time she's really okay, but when she sees one of these little girl toddlers, Sid's brain curdles."

"What you need, Edward Wilson, is a baby sister," said his mother.

Eddie looked up at his mother with big round eyes and said, "You mean we're going to get a baby?"

"No!" replied his mother. "It might turn out to be another boy, and four boys are enough around this house."

"But you do like us, don't you, Mother?" Eddie said.

Mrs. Wilson put her arm around Eddie's shoulder and said, "I love you and you know it, and I love Rudy and Joe and Frank and they know it."

Eddie reached into the cookie jar again. "I wish I could think of some way to make some money," he said, "just enough to buy a new baseball mitt. If I had an animal it could have babies and I could sell them. 'Course I don't suppose anybody would want to buy any baby skunks, but they're awful cute."

"I should say not!" his mother exclaimed. "And if any of your animals ever had babies, you would never part with one of them. I know you, Eddie! The house would be full of baby animals all growing up. The day would come when we'd have to move out of this house. There wouldn't be room for us and all the animals."

"Oh, Mother! You exaggerate," said Eddie.

His mother laughed. "It's too bad we don't live near a zoo, so you could get a job in the zoo," she said.

"That would be swell!" Eddie responded. "Then maybe I could learn to be a lion tamer. You know, like in the circus. A man goes in the lion's cage with just a chair. He holds it in front of him and he tames that lion." Eddie picked up a small wooden chair and held it out. "Like this," he said. Then he added, very sadly, "All I've got is a chair."

"Well, go sit on it," said his mother, "and stop eating the cookies."

"I guess I'll go over and see what Annie Pat is doing," said Eddie. "Annie Pat's a good egg. I guess I'll go over and see what she's up to. She's always making something. Something fabulous.

That's what she always says, *fabulous*! Good old 'Peanut-butter-side-up' Annie Pat. You know, Mama, if I drop my bread and peanut butter, sure as shooting it falls on a lot of ants, but if Annie Pat drops her bread and peanut butter it just falls on a paper napkin. My peanut butter sticks to the ants, but Annie Pat's is as good as new."

Mrs. Wilson laughed and said, "Well, I'll bet anything that when she picked it up she would give half of it to you."

"That's right," Eddie agreed. "Annie Pat always divvies with me."

As Eddie went out the back door he called goodbye to his mother.

"Be back for lunch at one," his mother said.

"Okay," Eddie replied, as he mounted his bicycle.

It didn't take Eddie long to pedal over to Anna Patricia's. He placed his bicycle beside the Wallaces' garage and went to the front door. He rang the doorbell, and in a moment the door was opened by Anna Patricia.

"Hi, Eddie," she said. "Come on in. I've got something fabulous to tell you."

"What is it?" Eddie asked.

"I'm making money," Anna Patricia replied.

"You're making money!" exclaimed Eddie, his eyes popping. "What are you making it out of?"

"I'm not making it out of anything," said Anna Patricia. "I'm an artist and I'm selling my paintings."

"You're kidding," said Eddie.

"I am not, Eddie Wilson! I just sold a painting of my Aunt Mabel's dog for fifty cents. I'll show it to you. It's in my studio."

"In your what?" asked Eddie.

"My studio," replied Anna Patricia. "All artists have studios. It's where they paint their paintings. Come on." Anna Patricia led the way through the house and out the back door. Eddie followed her to the garage. There was a small door right beside the big overhead door. "This is the door of my studio," said Anna Patricia, opening the door. The two children went inside. Then Anna Patricia waved her hand and said, "This is my studio."

"It looks like the garage to me," said Eddie.

"That's just because you have no imagination," said Anna Patricia. "When you have imagination, a hut can be a palace. The trouble with you, Eddie, is you have no imagination."

"Well, I have enough imagination to know that I wouldn't like to live in a hut and imagine it was a palace. Do you know what huts are like? No refrigerators, no dishwashers, no washing machines!" Eddie waved his arms around and continued, "No bathtubs! Do you know that? No bathtubs. How could you take an imaginary bath in an imaginary bathtub? Just tell me that."

"Eddie," said Anna Patricia, very quietly, "we are not talking about imaginary bathtubs. Did I say anything about an imaginary bathtub? The trouble with you is, you let your imagination run away with you."

"You said I didn't have any," said Eddie.

"Well, you should have it about my studio and not about bathtubs," said Anna Patricia.

"Okay," said Eddie. "I'll play the game. This isn't a garage. This is a studio."

"That's right," said Anna Patricia. "I just let my father keep his car in my studio."

Eddie fell over the lawn mower. "And the lawn mower," said Anna Patricia. Eddie knocked over a rubbish can. "And those rubbish cans," said Anna Patricia. "After all, you have to keep the rubbish cans someplace."

"Sure," Eddie agreed. "Studio's a good place for rubbish cans."

"Well now," said Anna Patricia, when they had climbed over more garden tools, a bag of fertilizer, and a pile of flowerpots, "this is where I have my easel and here is the painting that I just sold."

Eddie looked at the painting that was standing on the easel. A large head of a cocker spaniel looked back at him. The eyes were very bright and the ears hung down, long and curly. The mouth had a pleased expression as though the dog had just scared the robins out of the garden.

"It's the first painting I ever sold," said Anna Patricia, with a note of pride in her voice. "My Aunt Mable gave me fifty cents for it."

"It's a big painting for fifty cents, Annie Pat," said Eddie. "Did you paint with real oil paints?"

"That's right," Anna Patricia replied.

Eddie examined the painting more carefully. "And it isn't painted on paper, is it?" he said.

"Oh, no," Anna Patricia replied. "It's canvas board."

"Just like a real artist," said Eddie, "but I never saw an orange cocker spaniel before."

"That's because you never looked at a brown cocker spaniel when the sun was shining on it," said Anna Patricia.

"Sure I have," Eddie replied. "Do you think I only look at dogs when it's raining or when it's dark?"

"Well, maybe you look at them," said Anna Patricia, "but you don't see them."

"I don't see them!" exclaimed Eddie. "What do you mean, I don't see them? I've been seeing dogs all my life. You know I've found loads of dogs, lost dogs! How could I find them if I didn't see them? Answer me that, Annie Pat."

"But if you really had seen them you would know what color they are when the sun shines on them," said Anna Patricia. "My art teacher says nothing is the same color in the sunshine as it is in the shade."

"Huh!" said Eddie. "Dogs that change color! I never heard of that. An orange cocker spaniel!"

"Well, Eddie, don't forget I sold it for fifty cents," said Anna Patricia. "You never painted a cocker spaniel any color at all for fifty cents."

Eddie stood looking at the painting. At last he said, "Tell you what, Annie Pat, if your Aunt Mabel paid you fifty cents for this painting of her dog, maybe some other people would pay you to paint their dogs."

"I thought of that," replied Anna Patricia, "but I wouldn't know how to find out."

"Oh, that's easy," said Eddie. "All you have to do is take this painting around and show it to people who have dogs."

"What would I say?" Anna Patricia asked.

"You just say, 'Good morning! I paint dogs.' Then you hold up the cocker spaniel and you say,

'Would you like to have your dog painted?' Then they say, 'How much do you charge to paint my dog?' and you say, 'Fifty cents.' "

"Oh, I couldn't do that!" said Anna Patricia. "Not all by myself. Anyway, the dogs won't hold still. My Aunt Mabel had to hold Laddie Boy all the time so I could paint him."

Eddie considered this for a moment and then he said, "Tell you what, Annie Pat! Maybe you and I could go into business. I could go with you and hold the dogs while you paint them."

"Would you ring the doorbells for me and say all that 'Good morning' business? I'm shy."

"You are?" said Eddie. "I never knew that, Annie Pat. Does it hurt when you're shy?"

"Well, it doesn't exactly hurt," she replied.

"How does it feel?" Eddie asked.

"Well," replied Anna Patricia, "all of a sudden you feel as though you didn't have any bones at all."

"Oh, that must be awful, Annie Pat," said Eddie. "How much will you pay me for being your bones and holding the dogs?"

"Fifteen cents?" said Anna Patricia, sounding a bit uncertain.

"Fifteen cents!" exclaimed Eddie. "For being your bones and holding the dogs? It's worth fifteen cents just to be your bones."

"Well, you don't want me to divvy with you, do you? Surely you don't want twenty-five cents, do you?" Anna Patricia asked.

"Well, no. I don't think you should give me half of what you make, but—well—what about twenty-two cents?"

"Okay," said Anna Patricia.

"We'll start tomorrow," said Eddie. "How about my taking the painting over to my house? I want to show it to my mother. She won't believe you can paint dogs if I don't show this to her."

Anna Patricia hesitated for a moment. Then she said, "Would you be very careful of it? You know, it belongs to my Aunt Mabel because she paid me fifty cents for it."

"Oh, sure," Eddie replied. "I'll be very careful of it."

As Eddie was about to leave, Anna Patricia handed the painting to him. "Now do be careful of it, Eddie," she said.

"Don't worry," Eddie replied. "I won't let anything happen to this painting."

When Eddie came home for lunch, he shouted, "Hi, Mother! Guess what! I've got a job. I'm a dog holder for Annie Pat. Annie Pat is painting people's dogs. I get the dogs and she paints 'em."

Mrs. Wilson laughed. "Eddie," she said, "you always have news."

Eddie held up the painting and said, "Just look at this! It's a painting of Annie Pat's Aunt Mabel's cocker spaniel. She paid Annie Pat fifty cents for it."

Mrs. Wilson looked at the painting and said, "That's quite a cocker spaniel!"

"If you're wondering why it's orange, it's because the sun is shining on it," said Eddie. "If the sun wasn't shining on it, it would be brown."

"Well, it certainly is orange!" said his mother.

"Oh, Annie Pat learns all about this sunshine business in her art classes," said Eddie.

Just then Eddie's big brother Rudy came in. He looked at the painting and said, "Wow! Who painted the sunburned dog?"

"Annie Pat," Eddie replied. "She paints dogs and she gets paid for painting them. She gets fifty cents. And guess what, Rudy?"

"I'll bet you're the dog holder," Rudy answered. Mrs. Wilson and the boys laughed.

"So Eddie and Anna Patricia are in business again," said Rudy. "This is going to be a busy summer!"

Chapter Two

EDDIE GOES TO A PARTY

EDDIE stood the painting of Laddie Boy on top of a pile of newspapers that were on a table in his father's study. He left it propped against the wall. Then he went to eat lunch with his mother and Rudy at the kitchen table. The twins, Joe and Frank, were having lunch at a friend's house. "What are you boys doing this afternoon?" Mrs. Wilson asked.

"I'm playing tennis over at the Community Center," said Rudy.

"I'm going swimming in the Community Center pool," said Eddie. "What are you going to do, Mother?"

"I'm going to make some lemon tarts for Sidney's mother," Mrs. Wilson replied. "She's having a tea party this afternoon and I promised to make the tarts."

"You mean those little bitty ones?" said Rudy.

"That's right," his mother answered.

"Make some extra for us, won't you?" Eddie asked.

"Of course," said Mrs. Wilson. "Do I ever forget you boys when I'm making tarts?"

"Never!" the boys chorused.

After lunch, Rudy took up his tennis racket. Eddie said, "Wait for me, Rudy. I have to get my swimming trunks." Eddie ran upstairs. When he came down, Rudy was waiting for him in the hall. The boys called good-bye to their mother and went out the front door. They banged the door behind them and it shook everything in the hall and in their father's study. It shook Aunt Mabel's cocker spaniel and his bright face fell flat on the top of the pile of newspapers.

Mrs. Wilson made the lemon tarts and put them in the oven. Then she picked up the morning paper, which had been lying on a chair in the kitchen, and carried it into Mr. Wilson's study. She sat in an easy chair and read the paper until she heard the bell ring on the stove. She knew then that it was time to take the tarts out of the oven. Mrs. Wilson got up and threw the paper on top of the pile of newspapers. She noticed that the pile was topped by a board that looked like a piece of gray cardboard. She said to herself, "This pile of papers is beginning to look like a pile of rubbish. I must get one of the boys to take them down to the cellar, for the rubbish collection tomorrow."

Mrs. Wilson went into the kitchen and took the tarts out of the oven. She set them aside to cool.

About three o'clock the twins came in. Mrs. Wilson called out, "Joe! Please take that pile of news-papers down to the cellar and put them with the rubbish to go out tomorrow."

"Sure," said Joe, "right away." Joe took the pile of papers down to the cellar. Then he came upstairs again.

Frank came into the kitchen. "Oh! Lemon tarts!" he exclaimed. "I could eat all of them."

"Well, you're not going to," said his mother. "These are for Mrs. Stewart's tea party."

"Oh, Mother! All of them?" said Frank.

His mother laughed and said, "No, I have saved some for you boys."

"Good," said Frank. "I'll have mine now." He popped a tart into his mouth.

"I want to put these tarts on something flat," said his mother. "I wonder whether you can help me find something."

"How about a cookie sheet?" Frank suggested.

"No," said his mother, "if I put them on a cookie sheet Mrs. Stewart will have to return it, and she will feel that she has to put something nice on it."

"Well, fine," said Frank. "Maybe she'll put a whole roast turkey on it."

Mrs. Wilson laughed. "Frank," she said, "you are the limit! Your arms and legs must be hollow to hold all the food you eat." Frank licked his fingers and grinned at his mother.

Then Mrs. Wilson said, "I think I saw a nice piece of cardboard in with those newspapers that Joe has just taken down to the cellar. See if you can find it."

Frank went down to the cellar. He found the pile of newspapers. Picking up the one on top of the pile, he uncovered the board. It looked like a heavy piece of gray cardboard to Frank, just as it had to his mother. He picked it up and without examining it he carried it up to the kitchen. "This it?" he asked.

"That's it," Mrs. Wilson replied. "Put it right down on this piece of foil." Frank put it down and Mrs. Wilson proceeded to fold the piece of foil over the edges of the board. Then she placed another piece of foil on top of the board. She picked it up and turned it over, folding the edges neatly. Finally she fastened the edges down with sticky tape. Aunt

Mabel's cocker spaniel, Laddie Boy, was all wrapped up now in shiny foil.

"That's a nice tray you've made," said Frank. "It looks like real silver."

Mrs. Wilson arranged the tiny tarts on the tray. When she had finished there were thirty tarts in neat rows. "Now I'll put another piece of foil over them and you can carry them over to Mrs. Stewart. And don't drop them!"

"Horrors!" said Frank. A few minutes later, he went out of the kitchen with Anna Patricia's painting of Laddie Boy, holding up thirty lemon tarts. Frank delivered them safely to Mrs. Stewart.

Mrs. Stewart took them into her kitchen and lifted the cover off the tarts, and thought how nicely they were arranged. She decided to put the tray right on the dining room table rather than run the risk of breaking the tarts by placing them on a plate.

When Frank returned home he went upstairs, where his mother was changing her dress. He said to her, "Mrs. Stewart said to say thank you and she hopes you'll come over early for the party."

Just then Joe called to him, "Hi, Frank! It's time to go to Scout meeting." In a few minutes Mrs. Wilson was alone.

About four o'clock she went over to the Stewarts' house and soon other friends and neighbors began to arrive. Cars were parked along the street and in the driveway.

Shortly after his mother had left, Eddie came home. He hung his wet swimming trunks over the railing on the kitchen steps. His mother had left the back door unlocked and Eddie went into the house. He went to his father's study to take another look at Anna Patricia's painting. He looked at the table where he had left it and was surprised to find that the painting was not there. He looked around the room, but the painting was nowhere to be seen. Then he thought perhaps his mother had moved it. He looked in the living room. It was not there. He looked in the dining room and in the kitchen. He ran upstairs and looked through the bedrooms. The painting of Laddie Boy was not anywhere.

Eddie went back to the study. He looked behind

the table where he had left the painting. There was nothing there. Then it occurred to him that the pile of newspapers that had been on the table had evidently been carried down to the cellar. Eddie ran down the cellar steps and hurried to the pile of newspapers. He looked at the one on the top of the pile and saw that it was the morning paper. He began to go through the pile of papers. There was a great accumulation, for his father had neglected for several weeks to put the newspapers out with the rubbish. As Eddie neared the bottom of the pile, he became more and more troubled. If Anna Patricia's painting wasn't here, where could it be? he thought. He finally reached the very bottom of the pile. He straightened up and stood with his hands on his hips, wondering what to do next. He wondered where his mother was. He wished she would come home.

By the time he reached the top of the stairs he remembered that his mother had gone to Mrs. Stewart's party. He looked out of the dining room window and saw that there were quite a few cars parked in the Stewarts' driveway.

Eddie knew that he had not been invited to Mrs. Stewart's tea party, but he felt that he must see his mother and ask her about Anna Patricia's painting. He could not stand to wait until she came back. Eddie decided to go over to the Stewarts' and find his mother, but just as he started off he looked at his hands. They were black from going through the newspapers. He thought to himself, if he went in to a grown-ups' party with dirty hands, his mother would scalp him. He ran back and went upstairs and washed his hands. Then he decided to put on a clean shirt. Maybe if he dressed up he would be invited to have some refreshments! After he had buttoned his shirt, he decided to put on his Sunday trousers. Then he put on a gay bow tie, his plaid sports jacket, and his best shoes.

Eddie started off again. Just as he ducked between two parked cars in the Stewarts' driveway, he ran right into Anna Patricia and her mother. "Hi, Eddie," Anna Patricia greeted him. "You're taking good care of my Aunt Mabel's cocker spaniel, aren't you?"

"Oh, sure. Sure," Eddie replied.

"She paid me fifty cents for it, you know, and I wouldn't want anything to happen to it."

"Oh, sure not," said Eddie. "Neither would I." Eddie felt these words very deeply.

"Doesn't Eddie look nice?" said Mrs. Wallace. "You're all dressed for the party, aren't you?"

"Oh, I just put on these things, you know," Eddie replied. "Just these things. I just put 'em on. Well! I just thought I'd put 'em on."

"Anna Patricia is going to help Sidney pass the refreshments," said Mrs. Wallace, as they drew near to the front door.

"Are you going to help, too, Eddie?" Anna Patricia asked.

"I don't know," Eddie replied.

"Well, why were you invited to a grown-ups' party," asked Anna Patricia, "if you're not going to do anything?"

"I have to talk to my mother," said Eddie.

This seemed to be a perfectly good reason to Anna Patricia. After all, one never knew when one would suddenly have to talk to one's mother.

Eddie followed Mrs. Wallace and Anna Patricia into the Stewarts' living room. He saw his mother, standing with a group of friends, near the door. Mrs. Wallace and Anna Patricia stopped to speak to Mrs. Wilson and her friends. When Mrs. Wilson saw Eddie all dressed up in his best clothes, she was terribly surprised. "Why, Eddie!" she said. "What are you doing here?"

"Well, uh," said Eddie, "maybe I can help Sid and Annie Pat pass the refreshments." Mrs. Wallace and Anna Patricia moved into the room to speak to Mrs. Stewart. Eddie pulled his mother's sleeve and said, "Mother, I have to speak to you."

"I'm busy now, Eddie, with these friends," said his mother. "This is my son, Edward," she said to the friends.

Eddie said, "How do you do."

"Why don't you go find Sidney?" his mother said, but Eddie stayed beside his mother. He did not want to find Sidney. He just had to find out what happened to Anna Patricia's painting.

In a few minutes, Mrs. Wilson's friends left her. "Mother!" said Eddie. "Listen, Mother, what—"

But at that moment, Anna Patricia came up to Mrs. Wilson and said, "Did Eddie show you the painting I did of my Aunt Mabel's cocker spaniel?"

"He did indeed," Mrs. Wilson replied. "You paint very well, Anna Patricia."

"Thank you," said Anna Patricia. "Eddie's going to get me some dogs to paint. He's going to show Laddie Boy to people who have dogs."

"That's very nice," said Mrs. Wilson. Then she looked down at Eddie and said, "Now, Eddie, what did you want to ask me?"

"Oh, uh, nothing, Mother. Just something. I'll see you again," said Eddie. Some more people came up to speak to his mother.

"Come on over to the table, Eddie," said Anna Patricia, "there are some wonderful goodies."

On the way to the table Eddie came upon Sidney's mother. "Hello, Mrs. Stewart," he said. "I just came over to see my mother about something."

"Well, stay and help Sidney and Anna Patricia," said Mrs. Stewart. "They will be glad to have two helping hands."

Eddie went to the table where Sidney and Anna Patricia were sampling some chocolates. "Hello, Eddie," said Sidney, "have a chocolate." Eddie ate a chocolate and Sidney handed him the tray with his mother's tarts on it. "Pass these around, Eddie," she said.

Eddie took the tray and started to pass it around among the guests. When he reached his mother he whispered to her, "Where's Anna Patricia's painting of the cocker?"

"Why, Eddie! I haven't any idea," his mother answered. "Where did you put it?"

Before Eddie could reply, Anna Patricia came bustling up and said, "Oh, Mrs. Wilson! Your tarts look fabulous!"

"I'm glad you like them, Anna Patricia."

Eddie walked off with what remained of the tarts. Soon they were all gone and he was back with his mother with the tray in his hands. "I put it on the table on top of the pile of newspapers," Eddie whispered to her.

"Joe took the newspapers down to the cellar," said his mother.

Suddenly Anna Patricia was at Eddie's elbow again. "Eddie," she said, "if you're through with that tray, I'll take it." Eddie handed the tray to Anna Patricia. Anna Patricia would have been very much surprised if she had known that she was holding the painting of Aunt Mabel's cocker spaniel all wrapped up in shiny foil. She carried it to Sidney and said, "What shall I do with this? The tarts are all gone now."

"Put it in the kitchen," said Sidney. "Mrs. Green is there washing up teacups." Mrs. Green had come to help with the dishes. "She'll tell you what to do with it."

Anna Patricia carried the tray into the kitchen and showed it to Mrs. Green. Mrs. Green said, "You might as well throw that into the wastepaper basket."

"It's too big to go in," said Anna Patricia.

"Well, stand it down beside the basket," said Mrs. Green. "I'll throw it out later." Anna Patricia placed the tray beside the wastebasket and went back to the living room.

In a few minutes Sidney's little cousin Susie, who

had been taking a nap, came down the back stairs into the kitchen. "I'm hungry," she said.

"I'll give you a glass of milk and a cookie," said Mrs. Green. While she was pouring the milk, Susie walked to the wastepaper basket and picked up the shiny tray that was standing beside it. "Pretty!" she said. "Awful pretty!"

"Sit up to the table," said Mrs. Green, "and I'll put your glass of milk and cookie on that nice tray." Susie sat at the kitchen table and drank her milk and ate her cookie. When she had finished she climbed down. She pushed the glass off the tray and took the tray in both hands. She began to tear the foil off. "Now," said Mrs. Green, "if you are going to make a mess with that, you had better go upstairs to the playroom. You can pull it all off. Won't that be nice?"

"Yes," replied Susie, as she carried Anna Patricia's painting, just beginning to show through the torn foil, up the back stairs.

Meanwhile Eddie was back, whispering to his mother. "I went through all of those papers, Mother," he said. "I couldn't find it."

Just then Mrs. Stewart called to Eddie and said, "Oh, Eddie. I don't see Sidney around, so will you run upstairs and see if Susie is all right? She's been asleep for a long time."

"Sure," said Eddie, starting off at once.

He ran up the front stairs. He looked in Sidney's room, where he knew Susie would be sleeping, but she was not there. Then he went to the playroom. Sitting in the middle of the floor was Susie, surrounded by strips of shiny foil. To Eddie's amazement, she was holding the painting of Aunt Mabel's cocker spaniel in her hands.

"Nice doggie," Susie chortled.

"Hey!" Eddie cried, pouncing upon it. "Where did you get that?" In a flash Eddie grabbed the painting out of Susie's hands, flew down the stairs, and bolted out of the front door.

Susie yelled. She screamed. All of Mrs. Stewart's guests stopped talking. Susie went on screaming. Sidney appeared. "Sidney," said her mother, "do go see what's the matter with Susie."

Sidney and Anna Patricia both went upstairs to

Susie. "What's the matter, Susie darling?" Sidney asked.

"Bad boy took doggie!" Susie yelled.

"Now, Susie, darling," said Sidney. "Don't be silly. There isn't any doggie around here. You know there isn't any doggie. Now be a good girl and stop crying. Come downstairs and have a cookie."

Meanwhile, Anna Patricia was gathering up the strips of foil. "Where do you suppose she got all of this foil?" she said.

When the children came into the living room Anna Patricia said to Sidney, "I wonder where Eddie is?"

"I don't know," Sidney replied. "I guess he went home."

With her mouth full of cookie, Susie said, "Bad boy, took Susie's doggie."

"She must have been dreaming," said Sidney to Anna Patricia. "She was asleep a long time. She must have been dreaming."

Chapter Three

PAINTING BUSTER

Early the next morning Eddie arrived at Anna Patricia's on his bicycle. He found Anna Patricia eating her breakfast. "You all ready to paint?" he said.

"I'll be ready to paint by the time you bring the first dog," Anna Patricia replied.

Anna Patricia's mother was reading the morning paper. "You must have gotten up early this morning, Eddie," she said. "Did you take time to have your breakfast?"

"Oh, yes," Eddie replied, "but I like to start work early."

"Do you have time to eat a cinnamon bun?" Mrs. Wallace asked.

"Thank you," said Eddie, "that would be very nice."

"How about a glass of milk with it?" said Mrs. Wallace. "Can you take time?"

"I guess so," said Eddie. "I'd like a glass of milk, thank you."

Eddie sat down at the table and broke his cinnamon bun in half. "You know, Annie Pat," he said, "I can't go on my bike to find these dogs for you to paint, because I'll have to walk them from their houses to your garage."

"Studio!" said Anna Patricia.

"Oh, sure," said Eddie. "I'll have to find dogs right around here, so I won't have to walk 'em too far."

"Mrs. Martin lives right up the street," said Anna Patricia, "just about two blocks. She has a very nice cocker spaniel. He's black."

"Aren't you going to paint anything but spaniels?" Eddie asked.

"Of course," Anna Patricia replied. "You can bring any kind. Any kind at all."

Anna Patricia's mother put the paper down and said, "Now, children, I hope you won't make a nuisance of yourselves with this dog painting business."

"Oh, no, Mother," said Anna Patricia. "We'll just ask the people nicely, and if they don't want their dog painted, we'll just go away. Won't you, Eddie?"

"That's right," said Eddie.

Eddie finished his milk and cinnamon bun and said, "Maybe it would be a good thing to begin with a cocker, 'cause you already did one and I can show it to Mrs. Martin."

Anna Patricia and Eddie left the table and went to the garage. Anna Patricia handed Eddie the painting of her Aunt Mabel's dog and said, "Now do be careful of this painting, Eddie. Remember, my Aunt

Mabel has paid me for it so it really doesn't belong to me."

"I'll be careful of it," said Eddie, putting the painting under his arm. "You get yourself set up to paint because I think I'll be back very soon with that cocker."

"I'll be ready," Anna Patricia replied, as Eddie walked away.

Eddie knew where Mrs. Martin lived. She lived in the biggest house on the street. When he reached the house he went to the front door and rang the bell. At once Eddie heard a dog bark. In a moment the door was opened by Mrs. Martin. "Be quiet, Buster!" she was saying to the dog. "Be quiet!"

"Good morning," Eddie called out in a loud voice, in order to be heard above the barking. "I have a friend who paints dogs." Eddie held up the painting of Aunt Mabel's cocker spaniel. "Would you like to have your dog painted? Of course, not orange, because your dog is black. They cost fifty cents."

"Is it for charity?" Mrs. Martin asked. "For the hospital fund?"

"Oh, no," Eddie replied, "it's for Anna Patricia

and me. She's going to give me twenty-two cents a dog. We're just trying to make a little money."

"I see," said Mrs. Martin. She hesitated.

"Do you think fifty cents is too much?" Eddie asked.

"Well, fifty cents is quite a lot," Mrs. Martin replied.

"It's a genuine oil painting," said Eddie, "and very thick paint. I guess there is almost fifty cents worth of paint on this picture." Then, looking at the black dog, he said, "I guess black paint costs a lot. I'll see that you get a nice shade of black."

"Very well," said Mrs. Martin. "Where is your artist friend?"

"She's right up the street in her gara—studio," said Eddie. "She's waiting for the dog."

"Who is the artist?" Mrs. Martin asked.

"She's Anna Patricia Wallace," Eddie replied. "She's very good at painting."

"Oh, I know Mrs. Wallace, and Dr. Wallace is my dentist," said Mrs. Martin. "I'll put the leash on Buster and you can walk him up to the Wallaces'."

"Thanks a lot, Mrs. Martin," Eddie said. "I'm crazy about dogs. I would have one myself only I can't decide what kind to get. I've had lots of strays, but of course I don't keep them because the owners always turn up."

Mrs. Martin fastened the leash to Buster's collar and said, "I'm happy to have Buster go for a walk. He'll be very good, I'm sure."

Eddie took the leash from Mrs. Martin and started off with Buster. At the end of the path Buster looked back at Mrs. Martin and she said, "Go along, Buster. Go along with the little boy."

Mrs. Martin closed the door. Buster took a few steps, then he stiffened his front legs. Eddie pulled on the leash. Suddenly Buster relaxed, the leash slackened, and Eddie almost fell on his face. It took Eddie about ten minutes to get Buster as far as the corner. He finally got him across the street, but before they had reached the middle of the next block, Buster lay down on the sidewalk. He lay down flat on his stomach, his front paws extended and his back paws stretched behind him. Eddie coaxed and coaxed

Buster just rolled his eyes up at Eddie. Buster wouldn't budge.

Finally Eddie decided to pick the dog up and carry him, but Buster would have none of that. Buster growled. Eddie leaned over and patted him. "Come on, Buster," he coaxed. "Come on. That's a nice dog." Buster liked this attention. He liked being patted. He liked being scratched on the head, but he would not let Eddie pick him up. He lay on the pavement like a rock. Eddie did not know what to do. At last he made up his mind that if Buster would not go to Anna Patricia, Anna Patricia would have to come to Buster. The question for Eddie to settle now was what to do with Buster while he went to get Anna Patricia. Eddie was certain that if he dropped the leash, Buster would run home. If he ran home, Mrs. Martin might decide not to have the painting made at all. Eddie looked around to see if there was something to which he could tie the dog. There was nothing.

Just then a little boy about four years old came around the corner on a tricycle. When he reached

Eddie he stopped. Pointing to Buster the boy said, "What's the matter with him?"

"He won't get up," Eddie replied.

"He's tired," said the boy.

Eddie held out the leash and said, "Will you just hold this leash until I get Annie Pat?"

"Who's she?" the child asked.

"She's going to paint a picture of this dog," said Eddie.

"Doesn't he want to have his picture painted?" the boy asked.

"He doesn't know about it," Eddie replied.

"Why don't you tell him?" was the boy's next question.

"Look," said Eddie, pushing the leash on the boy, "I'll go get Annie Pat and you tell him."

"Okay," the child replied. Getting off of his tricycle, the boy knelt down beside Buster. He had hold of the leash.

"Now don't let go of him," said Eddie.

"I won't," the boy answered.

Eddie ran as fast as his legs would carry him to

the Wallaces' garage. As he burst in the door Anna Patricia said, "Where have you been so long? Where's the dog?"

"I've got one!" Eddie cried. "I've got one up the street. He won't come. Come on! You can paint him there." Eddie grabbed up the easel and the paint box. "Bring the board and your brushes," he shouted as he started off again. "And don't forget the turpentine."

Anna Patricia came running behind Eddie. She

had the board and a wooden palette under her arm, the brushes in one hand, and the can of turpentine and a bunch of paint rags in the other.

When Anna Patrica and Eddie reached Buster there were five little children gathered around him. Tricycles stood all about.

"What are you going to do?" said one of the little girls as Eddie set up the easel.

"Going to paint this dog," Eddie replied.

"Oh! They're going to paint the dog!" the little girl called to the other children.

"What's that?" asked one of the boys as Anna Patricia squeezed some paint out of a tube and onto the palette.

"It's toothpaste!" another boy cried. "It's blue toothpaste!"

"It will make your teeth all blue," said another.

"It's pretty," said one girl, sticking her finger into the blue paint.

"Keep out of my paint," said Anna Patricia, looking at the little girl, who had already smeared the blue paint on her nose. Anna Patricia handed her a piece of paint rag and said, "Here, wipe the paint off your face."

The child wiped her face with the rag. She wiped everything except her nose. It remained bright blue.

"What's the red for?" asked another four-year-old, as Anna Patricia squeezed out some red paint.

"It's lipstick," said another, sticking her finger into the red paint.

Anna Patricia grabbed her finger and wiped off the red paint before it reached the child's lips.

"Now, Eddie," said Anna Patricia, "you will have to make the dog stand up. I can't paint him lying flat on the sidewalk."

"He won't stand up," Eddie replied.

"He doesn't want to have his picture painted," said the boy who had been holding the leash.

Anna Patricia wrinkled up her forehead and said, "Eddie, I can't paint him lying down. He won't look like a dog at all. He'll look like a rug on the floor."

Now all of the four-year-olds leaned over the dog and said, "Sit up, dog! Sit up!" Buster's head lay between his paws and he shut his eyes.

"He's asleep!" cried one child. The little children knelt down beside the dog and shouted, "Wake up, dog! Wake up!"

Anna Patricia looked at the children and said, "I'll never be able to paint with this mob of kids. Anyway, I have to have something to sit on. I can't paint standing up."

Eddie pointed to one of the tricycles and said, "Sit on that tricycle." Immediately the children jumped up.

"That's my tricycle!" one of the boys cried out. "I want to ride my tricycle." All of the children ran to their tricycles, climbed on them, and pedaled off.

"Now, if I had something to sit on, I could begin to paint," said Anna Patricia.

"Oh, sit on the pavement," said Eddie. "Don't be so fussy!"

"Well, all right," said Anna Patricia, sitting down, "but you will have to get that dog to lift his head up."

Eddie put his hand under the dog's chin and lifted it. "How's this?" he asked.

"His ears are lying on the pavement," said Anna Patricia.

"Can't you make believe his ears are hanging down?" asked Eddie.

"I'll try," Anna Patricia replied.

Anna Patricia was hard at work, sitting on the pavement, when the gang of tricycle riders returned. They all closed in on Anna Patricia.

"Why are you painting the dog blue?" cried one of the little boys.

"Because the sun is shining on him," Anna Patricia replied.

"The sun's yellow," said one of the children.

"Yes, the sun's yellow!" the others agreed.

"I never saw a blue dog!" cried another child.

"She's painting a blue dog! She's painting a blue dog!" the whole group began to sing out as they wheeled off on their tricycles.

"Annie Pat, you can't paint this dog blue. You just can't! We won't get paid the fifty cents if you do, because I told Mrs. Martin you would paint him a nice shade of black."

"Eddie, I have to paint what I see," said Anna Patricia. "Don't forget, I am the artist. You are the dog holder."

"Oh, boy," said Eddie. "We'll never get the fifty cents."

Every few minutes the four-year-olds were back, asking questions and sticking their fingers in the paint.

Suddenly Buster got up. Eddie had let go of the leash. He lunged for it, but the dog was too quick for Eddie. Buster shot up the street, dragging his leash. He dashed for his home with Eddie following at full speed. Mrs. Martin opened the door and Buster shot into the hall. "Well!" exclaimed Mrs. Martin. "Is the painting finished, and was Buster a good boy?"

"I guess the painting is almost finished," Eddie replied. "I hope you'll like it. It's a nice shade of black. Sort of blue."

"Well, Buster often looks blue to me," said Mrs. Martin.

Eddie ran back to Anna Patricia. "It's okay, Annie

Pat! It's okay!" he cried. "I guess we're going to get the fifty cents. Mrs. Martin says Buster often looks blue to her."

"You see," said Anna Patricia. "I'm an artist."

Anna Patricia delivered the painting while Eddie gathered up all of the painting supplies. When she returned, she gave Eddie twenty-two cents and said, "Mrs. Martin was very pleased with the painting."

"Thanks, Annie Pat," said Eddie, putting the money into his pocket. "Maybe someday your painting will be worth thousands of dollars."

"Oh, I don't think I'm that good," said Anna Patricia.

"Yes, you are," said Eddie. "You'll win a prize someday. You just wait and see."

Chapter Four

NOW IT'S A GERMAN SHEPHERD

A WHOLE week passed before Eddie and Anna Patricia set up dog painting once more. Anna Patricia had gone to visit her grandmother for several days.

One morning Eddie called Anna Patricia on the telephone and said, "Say, Annie Pat! We're not making much money painting dogs. How about it?"

"I know," Anna Patricia replied. "When are you going to bring one over to my studio?"

"How about this morning?" Eddie asked. "I know where there's a swell German shepherd. She belongs to a friend of my mother's, Mrs. Adams. She isn't very far from your house. Just about four blocks away. I think Mrs. Adams might like to have a picture of that German shepherd."

Eddie hung up and soon was off on his bicycle, heading for Anna Patricia's. He found her in the garage sitting at her easel, looking at a painting of a black and white spaniel. "When did you paint that?" Eddie asked.

"I did it while I was at my grandmother's," said Anna Patricia.

"That's great, Annie Pat," said Eddie. "Did you get fifty cents for it?"

"Yes," said Anna Patricia. "It's my cousin's dog, and my cousin paid me fifty cents and he said I could keep the painting. What do you think of that?"

"Didn't he like it?" Eddie asked.

"Oh, yes," Anna Patricia replied. "He just didn't have any place to hang it."

"I think you're mighty lucky to get fifty cents for nothing," said Eddie.

"For nothing!" exclaimed Anna Patricia. "Eddie Wilson! I worked hard for that fifty cents. You never painted anything, so you don't know what hard work it is to paint a spaniel."

"Well, have you got my twenty-two cents?" Eddie asked.

"Your twenty-two cents!" Anna Patricia cried. "You didn't do anything to earn twenty-two cents. You didn't get the dog. You didn't hold the dog. What makes you think you should get twenty-two cents?"

"Annie Pat, I've added it all up," said Eddie. "All together you've made a dollar and a half and you've only given me twenty-two cents. That's not much out of a dollar and a half."

"But Eddie, you only held one dog for me. That isn't very much dog holding."

"You know something, Annie Pat," said Eddie.

"You get mixed up about an awful lot of things, but you never get mixed up about money."

"Are you going to get the German shepherd?" asked Anna Patricia, changing the subject.

"Sure," Eddie replied. "Just wait until you see this dog. She's beautiful."

"Go ahead, bring her," Anna Patricia answered. "I'll be all ready when you get here."

"Okay," said Eddie.

"Don't let this dog lie down on the pavement," said Anna Patricia, "because I can't do my best work when they lie on the pavement. Keep her on her feet."

"Oh, we won't have any trouble with this dog," said Eddie.

Eddie left his bicycle against the wall of the garage.

With the painting of the orange cocker spaniel under his arm, he hurried to the house where the German shepherd lived. When he arrived he found Mrs. Adams at work in her garden.

"Hi, Mrs. Adams," said Eddie. "That's a beautiful German shepherd you have."

"Good morning, Eddie," Mrs. Adams replied, as the German shepherd came bouncing toward Eddie. Eddie stroked her and patted her, and Eddie and the dog were friends immediately.

"I never saw a more beautiful German shepherd," said Eddie. "What's her name?"

"Duchess," replied Mrs. Adams. "She is beautiful, isn't she?"

"Wouldn't you like to have a painting of Duchess?" Eddie asked. He held up the painting of the cocker spaniel and added, "My friend Anna Patricia Wallace painted this. They only cost fifty cents."

Mrs. Adams took the painting in her hand and looked at it. Then she said, "Has your friend ever painted a German shepherd?"

"Not yet," replied Eddie, "but she would like to."

Mrs. Adams thought for a moment. Then she said, "I don't believe so. Perhaps if she ever does a painting of a German shepherd you will show it to me. Then maybe I'll have Duchess painted."

"But if no one will let her paint their German shepherd," said Eddie, "she will never have a painting to show you. Wouldn't you let her paint Duchess, and then if you like it you could buy it?"

"Very well," said Mrs. Adams.

"Is it all right if I take Duchess over to Annie Pat's gara—studio?" Eddie asked. "She does her best work in the studio."

"Duchess doesn't like her leash," said Mrs. Adams. "She sometimes slips her collar when she has the leash on. You would have to be very careful. You see, Duchess is going to have puppies."

"She is!" Eddie exclaimed. "That's great. How many do you think she will have?"

"I don't know," Mrs. Adams replied. "You will be very careful of her, won't you?"

"I'll be careful, Mrs. Adams," said Eddie. "You needn't worry. I'll be very careful."

Mrs. Adams went into the house and got the leash. Duchess seemed delighted to be going for a walk. She leaped around with excitement. After some time, Mrs. Adams was able to fasten Duchess' collar.

Eddie started off, feeling very proud to be walking with a pedigreed German shepherd. When he came

through the door of the Wallaces' garage Anna Patricia exclaimed, "Oh! What a beautiful dog!"

"Mrs. Adams said you have to first paint the dog. Then if she likes the painting she'll buy it."

"Oh," said Anna Patricia. "Well, all right."

"We have to be very careful of her because she's going to have puppies," said Eddie.

"Oh, I'd love to have one of her puppies!" said Anna Patricia.

"You have to do a good picture of this dog," said Eddie. "Just remember my twenty-two cents. I don't want to hold this dog and not get my twenty-two cents."

Very soon it was clear that Duchess did not like her leash. Anna Patricia had not put a single stroke of paint on her board before Duchess slipped her collar. Eddie put it back. "I'll take the leash off," he said. "Mrs. Adams said she didn't like it."

Eddie worked with the hook but it was so stiff he could not unfasten the leash. "I can't get this off," he said.

"Maybe she won't do it again," said Anna Patricia,

always optimistic. A few minutes later Duchess slipped her collar again.

"Leave it off," said Anna Patricia. "You can put it back when you're ready to take her home."

"How am I going to hold her if she doesn't have either her collar or her leash on?" Eddie asked.

"She's so good," said Anna Patricia, "you don't have to hold her. Look how quietly she is sitting there."

The dog was indeed quiet. She sat on her haunches with her head held erect. She seemed to know that she was beautiful.

"Now see here, Annie Pat!" Eddie exclaimed. "I get twenty-two cents for holding the dogs. If I don't hold the dog you'll tell me that I didn't earn my twenty-two cents."

"I will not, Eddie," said Anna Patricia. "You know I'm always fair. You went over and got the dog."

"That's right," said Eddie. "I was your bones, wasn't I, when I went and showed Mrs. Adams the painting of the cocker?"

"Yep," Anna Patricia agreed. "That's worth eleven cents."

"Annie Pat!" exclaimed Eddie. "Now you're trying to rob me of eleven cents."

"I am not, Eddie," said Anna Patricia. "You know I wouldn't be so mean."

"Well, I just hope Mrs. Adams is going to buy this," said Eddie. "How is it coming? I hope you're not painting this dog pink or green or anything like that."

"I'm painting it dark gray," Anna Patricia replied.

"Oh, good," said Eddie.

"And lots of other colors," said Anna Patricia.

"What do you mean, lots of other colors?" said Eddie.

"I mix 'em up," Anna Patricia replied. "Red and blue and yellow."

"Oh, help!" Eddie cried. "If you're painting this dog red and blue and yellow, Mrs. Adams will never buy it."

"Don't be silly," said Anna Patricia. "I mix them

all together. After all, a German shepherd isn't just
one color. You can see that, Eddie. Look at
Duchess."

"Being an artist must be awful, Annie Pat," said
Eddie. "You have to know so much."

Anna Patricia brushed paint on the board. She
screwed up her face and looked at Duchess. She un-
screwed her face and looked at the painting.

"Why do you screw your face up when you look at
the dog?" Eddie asked.

"You always half close your eyes when you look
at what you're painting," said Anna Patricia. "I
learned that in my special art class. It helps you to
see what is important."

Eddie screwed up his face and looked at Duchess.
"It doesn't help me to see," he said.

"That's because you're not an artist," said Anna
Patricia.

Eddie got up and walked around where he could
see over Anna Patricia's shoulder. "Say, Annie
Pat!" he cried. "You better open your eyes, 'cause
that doesn't look like a German shepherd."

"What do you mean, it doesn't look like a German shepherd?" said Anna Patricia.

"I just mean it does not look like a German shepherd," said Eddie. "It looks like a cocker spaniel."

"Eddie Wilson!" cried Anna Patricia. "It couldn't possibly look like a cocker spaniel! Spaniels have long floppy ears."

"I don't care," said Eddie. "It looks like a spaniel without its ears. Maybe you've painted too many spaniels. Maybe you're just a spaniel painter. And her tongue looks like a red necktie."

Just then Duchess got up and walked to the door. She barked sharply and scratched on the door. "Maybe she wants to go out," said Eddie.

"Well, she can't go out now," said Anna Patricia. "I'm busy working on her nose."

"You might as well stop," said Eddie, "because you haven't got her nose long enough. She looks like a cocker."

Duchess barked again. "Maybe she has to go out," said Eddie.

"All right. Let her out," said Anna Patricia.

Eddie opened the door and Duchess bounded out. With great strides she leaped down the driveway. As Eddie watched he remembered the collar and leash. "Duchess!" he cried. "Duchess! Come back!"

Eddie took after the dog, but it was like running after the wind. Duchess had heard some dogs barking and she was running toward the sound. Then, to Eddie's horror, he saw the dogcatcher's van down the street. He saw a man with a great big net standing on the step on the side of the van. Duchess was racing toward the van. In a moment she would be abreast of it. Eddie followed, crying, "Duchess! Come back! Duchess!" Then Eddie's heart seemed to fly into his mouth, for he saw the man with the net jump off the wagon and run toward Duchess. Eddie stood as though frozen to the sidewalk as he watched the man scoop Duchess up in the net. In a moment Duchess was in the van behind the wire screening with the barking dogs.

Anna Patricia had now caught up with Eddie. "He's got her!" Eddie cried out. "The dogcatcher has Duchess!"

"Oh! Oh! This is awful!" Anna Patricia shrieked. "What will Mrs. Adams say?"

"She'll be furious," said Eddie. "Let's run and tell your mother. Maybe she'll take us to the dog pound to get Duchess."

"But my mother is out for the day," said Anna Patricia. "Don't you remember, the car isn't in the garage."

"We just have to get that dog back, Annie Pat," said Eddie. "Let's get on our bikes and see if we can find the dogcatcher's van. Maybe if we tell the man about Duchess and Mrs. Adams and everything, he will let Duchess out."

The children ran back to the garage to get their bicycles. "Be sure to take the collar and the leash with you," Anna Patricia called to Eddie.

"Oh, yes," said Eddie, grabbing them up.

The children started off in the direction that the dogcatcher's van had been taking when they had last seen it. As they crossed each street the children looked to the right and to the left, hoping to see the van. They rode around, block after block, but there was no sign of the truck. They were almost ready to give up the hunt when Eddie called out, "Listen! I hear a lot of dogs barking."

"So do I!" Anna Patricia called back. "Maybe it's the van!"

The children wheeled around and started at full speed up a narrow lane toward the sound of the barking dogs. It led them right into the street where Mrs. Adams lived. There was the dogcatcher's van, and there was Mrs. Adams sweeping her front pavement. Both children saw her. Without saying a word to each other, they turned and fled. Down the narrow lane they pedaled and around the block, hoping to meet the van. At last they reached a corner and saw it coming toward them. As it approached, the children waved their arms and shouted, "Please stop! Please stop!"

The van moved along without stopping. Eddie wheeled up beside the man who was standing on the step of the van and called to him, "Please, mister! You've got Mrs. Adams' German shepherd."

"Can't help it," the man replied. "There was no dog tag on that dog."

"But I have the dog tag right here," said Eddie, holding up the collar and the leash.

"You should keep it on her," the man replied.

"She slipped her collar," said Eddie.

Anna Patricia, riding beside Eddie, began to cry. "Oh, please!" she sobbed. "Please can't we have her back? She's going to have puppies. I was just painting her picture."

"I don't care what you were doing," the man replied. "These dogs are going to the pound."

At that moment a red police car appeared. The man on the step recognized the policeman in the red car and called out to him, "Hey, Kilpatrick! Will you chase these kids away? They're driving me nuts!"

When Eddie and Anna Patricia heard the name Kilpatrick, they looked over at the red car. There sat Mr. Kilpatrick at the wheel. Mr. Kilpatrick was the policeman who, when school was in session, took the children across the big wide street near the school. All of the children loved Mr. Kilpatrick.

"Mr. Kilpatrick!" Eddie cried out. "Oh, Mr. Kilpatrick!"

"Well, if it isn't Eddie Wilson!" Mr. Kilpatrick called back. "I might have known that it would be you following a gang of dogs, but usually a gang of dogs is following you."

"Oh, make them stop, Mr. Kilpatrick," Eddie cried. "Please make them stop!"

"Please, Mr. Kilpatrick!" Anna Patricia sobbed. "Duchess is going to have puppies."

"Stop!" said Mr. Kilpatrick to the driver of the van. The van stopped by the curb. Mr. Kilpatrick got out of the red car and the children got down from their bicycles. "Now tell me what it's all about," said Mr. Kilpatrick, "and Anna Patricia, stop your blubbering and blow your nose."

Soon Eddie had told the whole story. When he had finished, Mr. Kilpatrick said to the dogcatcher, "Bill, you better let me have the dog."

"What about the fee?" said the dogcatcher.

"How much is it?" Anna Patricia hiccuped.

"Two dollars," the man replied.

"I have a dollar and a half at home," said Anna Patricia.

"I have twenty-two cents here in my pocket," said Eddie.

"I'll make up the difference," said Mr. Kilpatrick, "and I'll advance the money." Mr. Kilpatrick handed the man two dollars.

"You'll have to take the responsibility for this, Kilpatrick," said the dogcatcher, as he let Duchess out of the van.

"I'll take it," the policeman replied. The load of dogs moved away.

The moment Duchess was released from the van, Eddie placed her collar around her neck. Then Eddie said, "Thanks, Mr. Kilpatrick. Here's my twenty-two cents."

"Oh, thank you, Mr. Kilpatrick!" said Anna Patricia. "If you will drive around to my house, I'll give you my dollar and a half."

"Mr. Kilpatrick, will you take my bike back to Annie Pat's, please," Eddie asked, "so I can walk the dog back to Mrs. Adams' house?"

"That I will," the policeman replied, and he lifted Eddie's bicycle into his car.

"I'll meet you back at my house, Mr. Kilpatrick," said Anna Patricia. "I'll go along slowly with Eddie."

When Eddie reached Mrs. Adams' house with Duchess, Mrs. Adams was sitting on her side porch. "Well, how is the painting?" she asked.

"The painting?" said Eddie. "Oh, the painting!"

"It isn't quite finished," Anna Patricia called from her bicycle. "I guess we'll have to have Duchess another day."

"That's right, Mrs. Adams," said Eddie. "Duchess certainly is a nice dog." He handed the leash to Mrs. Adams.

"I saw that awful dogcatcher's van go by," said Mrs. Adams.

"Oh, yes," said Eddie, patting Duchess on the head. "Good-bye, Mrs. Adams."

"Good-bye," Mrs. Adams replied.

Anna Patricia waved from her bicycle. "Good-bye, Mrs. Adams!"

As Eddie ran beside Anna Patricia's bicycle he said, "I think you should stick to spaniels, Annie Pat."

"The trouble with you, Eddie, is you don't have any perseverance," said Anna Patricia.

"I have so," said Eddie, "and it takes an awful lot of it to do dog holding for you, Annie Pat. And now I'm broke."

"Me too," said Anna Patricia, "after I pay Mr. Kilpatrick."

"The dog painting business isn't a very easy way to earn money," said Eddie. "I'll never be able to buy a baseball mitt."

"But think of Rembrandt," said Anna Patricia, pumping up a slight hill. "You know Rembrandt, who painted all those wonderful pictures in the museum? He didn't have a penny when he died. Not a penny! But just look. Now, after about three hundred years, his paintings are worth millions of dollars."

"Well, okay," said Eddie. "But I don't want a baseball mitt three hundred years from now. I want it this summer."

"Oh, Eddie," said Anna Patricia. "You're so greedy."

"Greedy!" exclaimed Eddie. "Greedy! Just because I don't want to wait three hundred years to get a baseball mitt!"

"You'll just have to find some more dogs," said Anna Patricia. "All we need are dogs."

"Well, I sure hope business picks up," said Eddie, as they turned into Anna Patricia's driveway where Mr. Kilpatrick's red car was waiting.

Chapter Five

BOODLES' BIRTHDAY PRESENT

IT TOOK Eddie and Anna Patricia several days to recover from their experience with the dog-catcher. They felt somewhat shaken up.

One morning not long after the terrible chase, Eddie went to see his friend Boodles. He was not at home when Eddie arrived, but Eddie soon found him in one of the neighbors' yards. Boodles was busy focusing a camera.

"Hi, Boodles," Eddie called out, as he got off his bicycle. "Where did you get the camera?"

Boodles looked up and said, "Hello, Eddie. I just got this camera for my birthday."

"Oh, great!" Eddie exclaimed.

"I'm going to take a picture of Mrs. Brownley's dog," said Boodles. "The Brownleys live in this house. They just got the dog. He's an Airedale and you'll never guess what his name is! Give a guess. Just for fun, give a guess."

"Brownie!" said Eddie, without hesitating a moment.

Boodles laughed. "You're real smart, Eddie," he said. "Real smart."

"Where is he?" Eddie asked.

"Mrs. Brownley is going to let him out in a minute," Boodles replied. "He's just a puppy and pretty frisky."

"Do you think Mrs. Brownley would like to have the dog's picture painted?" Eddie asked.

"Painted?" said Boodles. "Oh, I don't think so

Eddie. After all, she's going to have a nice photograph of him. I'm going to be real careful and get a good one. You know how it is, when you're getting paid for taking pictures, they have to be good. I'm lucky. If I didn't have my father to develop my films, I wouldn't make as much money."

Eddie looked hard at Boodles and said, "What do you mean, getting paid?"

"Well, you see, I got this swell idea! Now that I have this camera, I can make some money taking pictures of people's dogs," Boodles replied.

"Boodles!" Eddie shouted. "You can't do that! You just can't do that!"

Boodles looked at Eddie in amazement and said, "Why not? This is a good camera. I know how to work it, and I like dogs. So why can't I do it?"

"Because you'll use up all the dogs around here and take business away from Annie Pat and me. We're in business," Eddie replied.

"What business?" Boodles asked.

"Painting dogs," Eddie replied. "She paints 'em and I—"

Suddenly the back door of the house was opened

and an Airedale puppy shot out into the yard. First he jumped all over Eddie and then he jumped all over Boodles. After that he ran around and around and around as though witches were after him.

Boodles put his camera down on an iron bench and chased after the dog. "Help me catch him, Eddie!" he called out.

Eddie just stooped down and called out, "Here, Brownie. Come here, Brownie."

Brownie stopped racing around and came to Eddie. "It's a funny thing," said Boodles, "dogs always come to you, Eddie."

Eddie laughed. "I know," he replied. "Maybe I smell like a bone."

This made Boodles laugh. Then he said, "Now, Eddie, you hold him and I'll snap the picture."

"Look here, Boodles!" Eddie exclaimed. "I'm not holding any dogs for you. I hold dogs for Annie Pat, and I get paid for holding dogs."

"How much do you get?" Boodles asked.

"Twenty-two cents a dog," Eddie answered.

"Twenty-two cents!" Boodles cried. "I only get

ten cents for a picture. How much does Anna Patricia get for a painting?"

"She gets fifty cents," Eddie replied.

"That's a lot," said Boodles. "Of course, I can take a lot of pictures real fast. I'm going to go all around the neighborhood this morning and take pictures of dogs. I guess I'll make a good bit of money."

"But, I tell you, Bood, you can't do that," said Eddie, very much distressed. "If people buy your photographs, they won't buy Annie Pat's paintings."

Brownie was racing around and around the yard again. Boodles watched him. "Eddie," he said, "how can I take this dog's picture, if you won't hold him?"

"I don't know," Eddie replied, "but I'm not holding dogs for anybody except Annie Pat."

"I think that's pretty skunky of you," said Boodles. Boodles looked very glum as he watched the dog running about.

Eddie looked glum, too. Finally Eddie said, "Tell you what, Bood. If you will take pictures of cats, I'll hold cats. I'll hold cats, but I won't hold dogs."

Boodles shook his head, so Eddie continued. "You

have a lot of trouble with dogs, Bood. You have to watch out for dogcatchers. You don't have any trouble with cats 'cause there aren't any catcatchers."

Boodles fingered his camera and watched Brownie. "It's only fair," said Eddie. "Annie Pat and I chose dogs before you ever got your camera."

After a while Boodles said, "Well, okay. But what about the dogs the people won't let Anna Patricia paint? Can I take their pictures?"

"I'll have to ask her," said Eddie, walking toward the back door. Then he asked, "How much do I get for holding a cat?"

"Do you mean I have to pay you for holding a cat?" Boodles asked.

"It wouldn't be fair if Annie Pat paid me twenty-two cents for holding dogs and I held your cats for nothing," said Eddie.

"Well, I can't pay you very much," said Boodles. "Just remember, I only get a dime."

"Couldn't you pay me two cents a cat?" Eddie asked.

Boodles thought this over. Finally he said, "Okay, two cents a cat."

"Three cents, if they scratch," Eddie said.

"Two cents!" Boodles cried. "Scratchers or not scratchers. Two cents!"

"Okay," said Eddie. "Let's see if Mrs. Brownley has a cat."

Boodles knocked on the door and when Mrs. Brownley opened it, she said, "Did you take the picture?"

"No, I didn't take it," Boodles replied. "Brownie is so frisky he won't hold still."

Mrs. Brownley looked at Eddie and Eddie said, "I'm Eddie Wilson. Wouldn't you like to have a real painting of Brownie? I have a friend who paints dogs. I can bring a painting that she made of her Aunt Mabel's cocker spaniel to show you. It's great, Mrs. Brownley. She only charges fifty cents and you get a real oil painting."

"I'm afraid Brownie would never hold still to have a painting made when he won't hold still for a photograph," said Mrs. Brownley.

"Oh, I could hold him," said Eddie. "I can hold any dog."

"Well, why don't you hold Brownie so Boodles

can take the photograph?" Mrs. Brownley asked.

"Well, you see, Mrs. Brownley, I'm a cat holder for Boodles and a dog holder for my friend, Annie Pat," said Eddie.

Mrs. Brownley just said, "Oh."

"Do you have a cat, Mrs. Brownley?" Boodles asked.

"No, I haven't any cat," Mrs. Brownley replied. When she saw how disappointed Boodles and Eddie appeared, she said, "I have a bird. Would you care to take a picture of the bird?"

"Oh, sure," said Boodles.

"I'll get the cage," said Mrs. Brownley.

While Mrs. Brownley was gone, Boodles said, "Look, Eddie, if you hadn't come along this morning I would have taken the picture of Brownie and made ten cents. You spoiled everything."

"You'd have to have a movie camera to take a picture of that dog," Eddie replied.

Just then Mrs. Brownley came back. She was carrying the birdcage. "Here's Pippa," she said.

Eddie held the screen door open for Mrs. Brownley, but as she came out she knocked the cage against the door. The jolt loosened the catch on the door of the cage, and it swung open. Pippa spread his tiny wings and flew into a lilac bush. "Oh, dear!" Mrs. Brownley screamed. "He's out!"

Boodles and Eddie stood as stiff as lead soldiers. Their mouths were wide open in surprise. "Don't move! Don't move!" said Mrs. Brownley to the boys. She began to make chirping sounds. Then she said, "Oh, he must come back to his cage. He must."

The pale blue feathers of the little parakeet showed plainly on the limb of the lilac bush. The dark green leaves made a beautiful background for the bird. Boodles lifted his camera to his eye and looked at the bird in his lens. He clicked the shutter just as Pippa flew into a tree that hung over the kitchen roof. "Now he's gone into the tree!" Mrs. Brownley cried. "Oh, what shall I do?"

"Maybe if we put the cage on the roof, he'll go in when he gets hungry," said Eddie.

"We'll have to get a ladder from the garage," said Mrs. Brownley.

The boys followed Mrs. Brownley to the garage. They helped her carry the ladder into the yard and place it against the side of the kitchen. "I can put the cage on the roof, Mrs. Brownley," said Eddie.

"Oh, thank you, Eddie," she replied.

Eddie mounted the ladder and Mrs. Brownley handed the cage to him. Eddie placed it on the roof. Mrs. Brownley continued to make chirping sounds. She tried talking to Pippa, but he paid no attention. He jumped from limb to limb, evidently enjoying his freedom.

Suddenly Pippa flew back down to the lilac bush. "Oh, dear," cried Mrs. Brownley, "now he's in the lilac bush and the cage is on the roof."

"I'll get it," said Eddie. Eddie went up the ladder again and brought the cage down. He put it on the garden table. Now Eddie noticed for the first time that there was a little mirror inside the cage. He picked up a twig and knelt down behind the table. Then he poked the mirror with the twig. The mirror glistened in the sunshine. Rays of light shot out from the surface. It caught Pippa's eye. For a few moments

he sat watching it, turning his head from side to side. Eddie kept moving the mirror very gently. Suddenly Pippa spread his wings and dived right into the cage. Mrs. Brownley quickly closed the door and made it fast. "Eddie," she cried, "that was a wonderful trick! You got my Pippa back! How can I thank you enough! Let's all go indoors and have some cookies and lemonade."

When the boys had finished their cookies and lemonade, Mrs. Brownley said, "Now, what about the photograph of Brownie?"

Boodles looked at Eddie and Eddie said, "Oh, okay. But after this it's cats."

"And birds," said Boodles. "I think I got a good shot of Pippa on the lilac bush."

The boys returned to the yard with Brownie. "I'll sit on the bench beside him," said Eddie. The moment Eddie sat down beside the dog, Brownie immediately wriggled into Eddie's arms.

Boodles held his camera to his eye. He could see Eddie with Brownie licking his cheek. "It looks great, Eddie," he said, as he snapped the shutter.

"Bring the pictures over when they're finished, Boodles," said Mrs. Brownley. "I'll buy the picture of Brownie and the one of Pippa." Then she turned to Eddie and said, "How much did you say your friend charges for a painting of a dog?"

"Fifty cents," Eddie replied.

"Well," said Mrs. Brownley, "if she would like to paint Brownie, I'll be happy to let her do it."

"Oh, that's super, Mrs. Brownley," said Eddie, as he put Brownie down. "I guess she better do it right here in your backyard, 'cause Brownie is certainly a frisky pup."

"When will you come?" Mrs. Brownley asked.

"Would tomorrow morning be all right?" asked Eddie.

"Yes," Mrs. Brownley replied. "I'll expect you tomorrow."

When Eddie parted from Boodles, he said, "Let me know when you want me to hold any cats, but not tomorrow. Tomorrow I'll be busy holding that dog for Annie Pat."

When Eddie reached home he telephoned to Anna

Patricia to tell her that Mrs. Brownley wanted her dog painted. Before he could say a word about it, Anna Patricia shouted into the telephone, "Oh, Eddie! Just wait until you see what I've painted. It's simply fabulous!"

"What is it?" Eddie asked.

"I'm not going to tell you," Anna Patricia replied. "You'll have to wait until you come over."

Anna Patricia was delighted to hear the news about Brownie. "I'll see you tomorrow morning," she said, "but I can hardly wait to have you see my new painting. You'll be surprised. It's fabulous! Good-bye."

As Eddie hung up the telephone, he put his hand to his head and said, "Now what?"

Chapter Six

A YANKEE-DOODLE DOG

THE following morning Eddie stood in front of Anna Patricia's easel looking at her most recent painting. He could hardly believe his eyes, for a large orange cat stared back at him. Eddie was speechless.

"Isn't she fabulous?" Anna Patricia exclaimed.

"Who's that?" Eddie managed to blurt out.

"Honeybun," Anna Patricia answered. "She's my Aunt Mabel's cat."

"You're not going to paint cats, Annie Pat!" Eddie cried. "You just can't paint cats!"

"What do you mean, I can't paint cats?" said Anna Patricia. "I've painted one. You're looking at it. And if you are wondering why it's orange, it's because—"

"I know," Eddie interrupted, "it's because the sun is shining on it."

"No!" Anna Patricia shouted, sounding triumphant. "It's because she's a marmalade cat."

"Well, I don't want any marmalade that color," said Eddie.

"We're not talking about marmalade, Eddie," Anna Patricia retorted. "We're talking about cats."

"We sure are talking about cats," Eddie replied, "and I tell you you have to keep out of the cat business. You have to stick to dogs."

"I'd like to know why," Anna Patricia said.

"Because Boodles has a new camera and he was all set to take pictures of dogs, and I told him dogs were our business and he would have to stick to cats.

I told him that I'm your dog holder and I could only hold cats for him."

"Is he going to pay you for holding cats for him?" Anna Patricia asked.

"Yepper!" Eddie replied. "Two cents a cat."

"That isn't very much," said Anna Patricia.

"Boodles only gets ten cents for a picture," Eddie answered. "Of course, he can take a lot of pictures in no time at all. The trouble with this painting business is it's so slow."

"That's because it's art," said Anna Patricia. "My Aunt Mabel paid me fifty cents for this painting of Honeybun."

"There you go again, making money when I'm not around," said Eddie.

Anna Patricia ignored this remark and said, "Did Boodles promise that he would leave the dogs for us?"

"Yes, he promised," Eddie replied. "Now you have to promise to leave all the cats around here for him."

"All right, I promise," said Anna Patricia, "but I do think my painting of Honeybun is fabulous."

Eddie looked at the painting and said, "What kind of a cat did you say it is? A jelly cat?"

"Jelly cat!" Anna Patricia roared with laughter. "It isn't a jelly cat. It's a marmalade cat."

"Oh, yes," Eddie laughed. "I knew it was something you put on bread." Then Eddie picked up Anna Patricia's can of turpentine and her paint box. "Come on," he said. "We have to get a move on if we're going to Mrs. Brownley's to paint her pup."

"All right," said Anna Patricia. "You take my easel on your bike and I'll bring everything else in my bicycle basket."

Eddie mounted his bicycle and Anna Patricia handed the easel to him, and the children started off.

When they reached Mrs. Brownley's house, Mrs. Brownley opened the door and said, "Good morning, Eddie."

"Good morning, Mrs. Brownley," Eddie replied. Turning to Anna Patricia, he said, "This is my friend who paints dogs, Anna Patricia Wallace."

"Good morning," said Anna Patricia.

"I'm glad to see you, Anna Patricia," Mrs. Brownley replied. "Come in, children." The children stepped inside.

Eddie held up the painting of Aunt Mabel's cocker spaniel and said, "This is the painting she did of her Aunt Mabel's cocker spaniel. Fabulous, isn't it?"

"Oh!" Mrs. Brownley exclaimed. Then she added, "It's really very nice."

"She's all ready to paint Brownie," said Eddie.

"Oh, yes," said Mrs. Brownley. "I put a chair in the yard for you, Anna Patricia."

"Thank you," said Anna Patricia. "I'm glad I don't have to sit on the grass because the dog might get into my paint."

"That's right," Eddie agreed. "Brownie is very frisky." Brownie was running circles around Eddie, letting out happy barks as Eddie tried to pet him.

"Now I have to drive into town," said Mrs. Brownley. "Will you be all right with Brownie?"

"Oh, sure," Eddie replied. "I won't let him out until Annie Pat is all set up."

"When you put Brownie back in the house, be sure to lock the kitchen door," Mrs. Brownley said.

"I won't forget," Eddie answered.

The children went to the yard. Anna Patricia was setting up her easel when Mrs. Brownley called good-bye to them.

Eddie watched as Anna Patricia squeezed paint out of the tubes. He liked to see the paint as it came out, all bright and shiny. First there was a big gob of red, then one of blue, and then one of white. As Anna Patricia picked up the tube of orange paint, Eddie said, "Go easy on that orange, Annie Pat. Remember, everything isn't orange."

Anna Patricia stood holding the tube of paint in her hand. "It's my favorite color," she said.

"That isn't any reason to slap it all over everything," said Eddie.

"Eddie Wilson, I do not slap paint around," said Anna Patricia. "I am a very careful artist."

"Well, I just hope you paint the dog brown," said Eddie, " 'cause that's what he is—brown. Just remember, his name is Brownie, and he isn't a jelly dog or a marmalade dog or anything like that. He's a brown dog."

"He isn't all brown," said Anna Patricia. "He has a lot of black on him."

"Okay, but paint him brown and black. Not orange and blue," said Eddie.

Still holding the tube of orange paint, Anna Patricia said, "Eddie! I am the artist. You are the dog holder. If I see the dog orange, I paint him orange. If I saw him red, white, and blue, I would paint him red, white, and blue."

"Well, Mrs. Brownley isn't going to pay you fifty cents for any Yankee-Doodle picture of her dog," said Eddie. "Red, white, and blue!"

"Oh, I didn't mean it," said Anna Patricia.

The children could hear Brownie barking to get out into the yard. "I'll let him out," said Eddie, "before he scratches all the paint off the door." Eddie opened the kitchen door and Brownie rushed out. Like a small bomb he shot toward Anna Patricia as she was about to squeeze out the orange paint. Then he rushed at the easel and knocked it over. Anna Patricia tried to catch it as it fell. Her palette flew out of her hand and turned upside down. It hit the dog right in the center of his back. Brownie rushed to the other end of the yard and around and around with large gobs of red, white, and blue paint sticking to his coat.

"Oh, look at him!" Anna Patricia cried.

Eddie was running after the little dog. "Here, Brownie! Here, Brownie!" he called out. Suddenly Brownie stopped short and came to Eddie. Eddie examined the dog's back. The red, white, and blue paint was stuck to his woolly hair. "Hand me your paint rag," Eddie called to Anna Patricia.

Anna Patricia handed the paint rag to Eddie, and Eddie rubbed it across Brownie's back, but instead of removing the paint, Eddie smeared it. Now Brownie had three broad stripes of paint across his back. They were red, white, and blue. "Oh," Anna Patricia cried, "you've made it worse! Now what shall we do?"

"We'll have to get it off," said Eddie.

"We can't use the turpentine," said Anna Patricia, "because it would burn his skin."

Eddie's forehead was all wrinkled up. "That's right," he agreed.

Just then Boodles came into the yard. "Hi!" he

cried. Anna Patricia and Eddie were too concerned over Brownie even to say hi. Boodles looked down at Eddie and Anna Patricia stooping beside the dog. "Well! Jumpin' grasshoppers!" he cried. "I didn't know you were really going to *paint* the dog. I thought you were going to paint a *picture* of him. He sure is a mess. I don't think Mrs. Brownley will like Brownie to be painted up like that. All that red, white, and blue! He looks as though he was going in the Fourth of July parade, but the Fourth of July parade is over."

"Oh, Boodles, stop your yapping," said Eddie. "Annie Pat's palette fell on the dog. It was an accident."

"We'll have to get the paint off of him," said Anna Patricia.

"You'll have to wash him," was Boodles' reply.

"Where?" asked Eddie, looking up at Boodles.

"We could do him in our laundry tub, I guess," Boodles answered.

"Let's do it right away," said Anna Patricia.

Eddie picked up Brownie, and Boodles led the way

to the basement door of his house. He pushed the door open and Eddie carried the dog to the laundry tub that was standing in front of a window. Boodles turned the spigots so that the water would be warm but not hot. Then he threw a cake of soap into the tub.

Meanwhile, Brownie was wiggling and squirming in Eddie's arms. When Eddie finally dropped the dog into the water, the whole front of Eddie's white shirt was purple, for the red, white, and blue paint had been rubbed together. "Oh, Eddie," Anna Patricia cried, "your shirt is an awful mess."

"Take it off," said Boodles. "Put it in with the dog." Eddie took his shirt off and put it in the tub with Brownie.

"Don't use my shirt as a rag to wash him," said Eddie. "It's one of my good shirts."

"We have to use something," said Boodles.

"Well, not my shirt," Eddie replied.

"Here's an old sponge on the windowsill," said Boodles "We can use this." Brownie was making it very clear that he did not want to have a bath. Eddie and Boodles both held him while Anna Patricia rubbed soap all over him. He wriggled and yapped and even howled, but the two boys held him firmly. As Anna Patricia worked on Brownie the bath water grew more and more purple.

After a little while Boodles' mother called down the cellar steps. "What's going on down there?" she said.

"We're washing Brownie," Boodles called out.

"Did Mrs. Brownley ask you to wash her dog?" his mother called back.

"No, but we have to because he got paint all over him—red, white, and blue—and we don't think Mrs. Brownley would like him red, white, and blue," was Boodles' reply.

"Certainly not!" his mother answered. "Those are no colors for an Airedale."

Finally Anna Patricia examined the results of her washing. "You can hardly see any paint now," she said, "but after I sponge him off we'll have to rub him dry with something."

"Mother!" Boodles shouted up the stairs. "Will you throw a towel down, please?"

"You are not going to dry that dog on one of my good towels," his mother called back.

"Well, we have to have something, Mother!" Boodles shouted up.

"I'll see what I can find," his mother replied. Soon she called down from the head of the stairs, "Here's an old pair of your father's pajamas."

Anna Patricia ran to the bottom of the stairs and picked up the pajamas. She handed them to Boodles, and Eddie lifted Brownie out of the tub. Water ran off of the dog and soaked Eddie's levis. Then Brownie jumped out of Eddie's arms and shook himself. Water flew everywhere. It flew all over the children and all over the floor. Brownie rushed around the basement, flinging water as he went. Boodles ran after him with the pajamas in his hand. Finally Eddie caught him, and Boodles set to work to dry him off. Anna Patricia stood by and watched the boys work.

After a while, Eddie looked at Boodles and said, "You know something, Bood? This dog holding business is a big job. It's almost time for lunch, and Annie Pat hasn't even begun to paint."

"That's right," said Anna Patricia. "We didn't come to wash a dog. We came to paint his picture."

"Well, it was your paint that got all over him," said Eddie. "I don't know why you don't get a camera like Boodles. It's much easier. All you do is snap and you've got it."

"But that isn't a painting," said Anna Patricia.

"It's a picture," said Eddie.

Just then Boodles' mother called down the stairs, "How about coming up for some lunch?"

"Lunch!" Boodles cried out.

"Oh, lunch!" exclaimed Eddie.

"Lunch!" Anna Patricia echoed. The children ran up the stairs, followed by Brownie.

Boodles' mother had set out sandwiches and cocoa for them, and they all sat down at the kitchen table. Little bites were fed to Brownie by each of the children.

When they had finished some fruit jello, Anna Patricia said, "Now, Eddie, I'll get your shirt out of the tub and it can dry on the fence while you hold Brownie for me."

"Okay," said Eddie.

It didn't take long for Anna Patricia to wring the water out of Eddie's shirt and hang it on the fence. When Eddie saw it he said, "That isn't my shirt. My shirt was white and that shirt is purplish."

"It got dyed," said Anna Patricia. "I think it is very pretty."

"I'm not going to wear a purplish shirt," said Eddie. "I'll carry it home and my mother will do it right."

Eddie caught Brownie, who was again racing around the yard. He took a firm grip on the dog and held him beside him on the garden bench.

Anna Patricia looked at Brownie and said, "I think I'll do Brownie side view."

"Good," said Eddie. "You'll only have to paint one eye and one ear."

Anna Patricia set to work while Boodles watched. After a while Eddie said, "How's it coming, Bood?"

"Pretty well," Boodles replied. "It looks a little like a horse now, but I think it's going to be good."

"What color is it?" Eddie asked.

"Well, sort of orange," Boodles replied.

Eddie shook his head. "She can't help it," he said. "It's her favorite color. You should see the cat she painted. She says it's a jelly cat. I mean a marmalade cat."

Boodles let out a yell that made Anna Patricia jump, Brownie bark, and Eddie lose his grip on the dog. "A cat!" Boodles yelled. "What do you mean, a cat? Cats are mine! You said they were. Cats are mine!"

"It's all right! It's all right!" Eddie cried out as he chased after Brownie. "I told her! I told her!"

"I only painted one," said Anna Patricia. "It was before I knew that cats were yours."

"Okay," said Boodles, as Eddie sat down once more with Brownie and Anna Patricia dipped her brush into the orange paint.

"Don't forget," she said. "Dogs are mine."

Chapter Seven

KING OF THE JUNGLE

VALUABLE PROPERTY

Aꜱ NNA PATRICIA had left the painting of Brownie on Mrs. Brownley's kitchen table with a note that read, "This is the painting of Brownie. I will come tomorrow for my fifty cents."

Mrs. Brownley was just finishing her breakfast when Eddie and Anna Patricia rode up on their bicycles. Brownie greeted them with barks, leaps, and licks. "Do you like the painting, Mrs. Brownley?" Eddie asked.

"I think Anna Patricia does very well," said Mrs. Brownley.

"Anybody would know it's an Airedale, wouldn't they?" said Eddie.

"Yes, indeed," Mrs. Brownley replied.

"And did you notice how nice and clean Brownie was when you came home?" Eddie asked. "We gave him a bath."

"You did!" exclaimed Mrs. Brownley. "Do you always wash the dogs before you paint them?"

"Not always," Anna Patricia said.

"This was just something special," said Eddie. "You see, Brownie got some paint on him and we didn't want to leave paint on him."

"I must say, it was very thoughtful of you to wash him," said Mrs. Brownley. "It saves me from having to do it. I have such a hard time keeping him still." Mrs. Brownley went into the other room and came back with her pocketbook. She opened it and took out a dollar bill. "I'm going to pay you fifty cents for the painting and fifty cents for washing Brownie," she said.

Anna Patricia and Eddie's eyes shone as Mrs. Brownley handed Anna Patricia the dollar bill. "Oh, thank you," said Anna Patricia.

"Thanks a lot," said Eddie.

The children soon said good-bye to Mrs. Brownley. When they were out of the house, Eddie said to Anna Patricia, "We have to get that dollar bill changed, because part of it belongs to me."

"I know," said Anna Patricia, "twenty-two cents for holding the dog and half of fifty cents for washing him."

"That's right," said Eddie. "But Boodles helped wash him, so we have to give him seventeen cents."

"I guess we'd better go to the bank," said Anna Patricia. They mounted their bicycles and rode to the bank. When they reached the bank, Anna Patricia said, "Now, you mind the bikes, Eddie, and I'll get the money." Anna Patricia went into the bank with the dollar bill. She came back with four rolls of pennies. She held them up and said, "I got pennies because it looks like more and it's easier to divide the money."

Anna Patricia sat down on the steps of the bank and Eddie joined her. As Anna Patricia broke the seal on the roll of pennies, she said, "Now, I'll give you twenty-two of these," but just as she said it, all of the pennies rolled down the steps of the bank.

"Old butterfingers!" cried Eddie. "Annie Pat, can't you do anything right?"

"I can paint dogs," Anna Patricia replied. "And I get money for painting them, too."

"Well, do you have to spill it all over the steps of the bank?" said Eddie, picking up pennies.

"I didn't spill it all," Anna Patricia replied. "I still have three rolls of pennies left."

"Well, give me my roll of twenty-five pennies," said Eddie, "before you break it. I want it wrapped up."

Anna Patricia was busy counting pennies. "How many did you find, Eddie?" she asked.

"Fourteen," Eddie replied.

"Well, I have eleven," said Anna Patricia, "so that makes twenty-five. We found all of them."

The children sat down on the steps again. Eddie held out his hand and Anna Patricia counted twenty-two pennies into his palm. "Now give me one of those rolls," said Eddie, " 'cause there's twenty-five cents more coming to me."

"But we each have to give Boodles eight and a half cents," said Anna Patricia.

"You can't divide a penny," said Eddie. "You must know that much, Annie Pat."

"Well, I'll give him nine and you give him eight, and that is very generous of me," Anna Patricia replied.

Anna Patricia handed over the roll of pennies to Eddie. "You know, I've been thinking," said Eddie. "Maybe we could make some extra money if we wash each dog before you paint it."

"Eddie, I am a dog painter," said Anna Patricia. "I am not a dog washer."

"Okay," said Eddie, "but I'll bet we could make more money washing dogs than painting dogs."

Eddie put his money in his pocket. As he did so, his hand touched a piece of paper. He pulled it out and said, "Oh, I almost forgot. I cut this out of the paper this morning. It says there's going to be an exhibition of paintings next week over at the Community Center. Maybe if you hang up one of your dog paintings, some people who have dogs would see it and ask you to paint their dog."

"Oh! That's wonderful!" Anna Patricia exclaimed.

"And there's something else," said Eddie. "It says there's going to be a prize for the best painting."

Anna Patricia shouted with glee. "What's the prize?"

"Twenty-five dollars!" Eddie replied.

"Twenty-five dollars!" Anna Patricia exclaimed. "Just imagine! Twenty-five dollars!" Anna Patricia jumped up. "Eddie!" she cried. "I'm going to get that prize! I'm going to put the picture of Aunt Mabel's cocker spaniel in that exhibition."

"Why don't you put in one that I held?" Eddie asked. "Why not the picture of Brownie?"

"Because Brownie only shows one eye and one ear," said Anna Patricia. "Aunt Mabel's cocker spaniel, Laddie Boy, has two eyes and two ears and his ears are so nice and curly. I think he would win the prize. He's really fabulous!"

"Well, maybe you're right," said Eddie. "Have you got a frame to put it in?"

"Oh," said Anna Patricia sorrowfully. "I never thought of that. I guess it has to have a frame.

"Of course," said Eddie. "It wouldn't get a prize if it wasn't in a frame."

Anna Patricia looked troubled. "I don't know where I can get a frame," she said.

"I guess if I looked through all of my valuable property that's in our basement at home, I might be able to find one. I just might," said Eddie.

"You mean in that mess of junk you have?" Anna Patricia asked.

"It isn't junk!" said Eddie. "It's my valuable property!"

Anna Patricia, recalling Eddie's willingness to call her father's garage her studio, said, "Do you really think you could find a frame for Laddie Boy in your pile of valuable property?"

"We can go look," Eddie replied. The children were off at once on their bicycles. When they reached Eddie's house, they stood their bicycles against the wall of the house.

Eddie's mother was in the kitchen shelling peas. "Hello, Anna Patricia," she said, when the children came in.

"Hello, Mrs. Wilson," Anna Patricia replied. "We've come to see if Eddie has a frame for my painting of my Aunt Mabel's cocker spaniel. He's going to look through his ju—valuable property."

"Annie Pat's going to hang her painting in an exhibition at the Community Center," said Eddie. "There's going to be a prize for the best painting."

"Well, in all of Eddie's junk there should be a frame of some sort," said his mother.

"Not junk, Mother!" Eddie called out as the children went down the cellar steps. "Valuable property!"

Eddie ran to the corner of the cellar where he kept

the treasures that he had collected. He began moving backs of old chairs, broken table legs, bent-up fire screens, works from old clocks, all kinds of broken-down motors, lamps, magazines, and various bits and pieces. Eddie had no idea what these were but he liked them. "I think I have a couple of frames back against the wall," he said.

"Where do you get all this valuable property?" Anna Patricia asked.

"Oh, I find it," Eddie replied. "The best time to find it is Clean-up Week. You should see the stuff people throw away Clean-up Week." Eddie plowed through his possessions. Finally he called out, "Here's one of them!" Eddie showed Anna Patricia a picture in a wide gold frame. The corners were broken and the glass was gone. Most of the gold had peeled off. Inside the frame was a faded picture of a great lion. Underneath, in dim letters, were some words. Eddie and Anna Patricia examined them. Then Eddie read, "King of the Jungle."

"Eddie, this frame is too big for my painting," said Anna Patricia. "I'm sure it's too big."

Eddie held up another frame. "This is the other one," he said.

"That's too small," said Anna Patricia.

"Well, Goldilocks! Those are all I have," said Eddie. "I can fix it in the big frame, though. I can put the picture of Laddie Boy right on top of that lion. It'll look good. It'll look like a picture in a museum."

"All right," said Anna Patricia.

"Let's take it over to your place and put the painting in the frame," said Eddie.

"Okay," said Anna Patricia, and she ran up the cellar steps. "We found a frame," she said to Mrs. Wilson.

"I thought you would," Mrs. Wilson replied. "Eddie has more junk than anyone I ever knew."

"Valuable property!" Eddie called back. His mother laughed.

It didn't take Eddie very long to put the painting of Laddie Boy in the frame. He fastened it into the top and sides of the frame with some small nails. It did not fit at the bottom, but it did cover the lion. All

that showed now were the words, *King of the Jungle*.

"I don't think that will do," said Anna Patricia. "Laddie Boy doesn't look like the King of the Jungle."

"It's so faded, I don't think anyone will see that," said Eddie. "When it gets up on the wall nobody will notice it. I think it looks great." Eddie stood admiring the results of all his effort.

"Do you know what, Eddie?" said Anna Patricia. "When I get that twenty-five dollar prize, I'm going to buy you a baseball mitt."

"You are?" exclaimed Eddie. "That sure is nice of you!"

"Well, you got this nice frame for me and you fixed Laddie Boy in it," said Anna Patricia.

"What will you do with the rest of the money?" Eddie asked.

"Oh, I've been thinking about it ever since you told me," said Anna Patricia. "I'm going to see if I can buy one of those little German shepherd puppies when Duchess has them."

Eddie was delighted with this idea. "That's what

I would do with the money," he said. " 'Course I
would buy a baseball mitt first."

When Eddie left to go home for his lunch, he
said, "I'll come over Monday morning to help you
take the painting to the Community Center."

"Okay," said Anna Patricia.

Eddie arrived early on Monday morning. "Are
you ready?" he said.

"Oh, yes," Anna Patricia replied. "Everybody
thinks the cocker looks wonderful in your frame, but
Mother says there will be lots of paintings and maybe
I won't get the prize."

"Sure you'll get it, Annie Pat," said Eddie. "I'm
beginning to like these bright orange dogs that you
paint. They show up so good."

Anna Patricia and Eddie took turns carrying the
painting. As the children neared the Community
Center, they could see several women holding paintings up in the air. Anna Patricia wondered what they
were doing with them. Then, as the children got
closer, they could see that the pictures were being
pinned to a clothesline.

Anna Patricia went up to one of the women and said, "I've brought my painting of my Aunt Mabel's cocker spaniel, Laddie Boy."

The woman looked down and said, "Oh, we can't hang it up in that frame. This is a clothesline exhibition. The paintings have to be pinned to the clothesline."

Anna Patricia looked very disappointed, but Eddie spoke up and said, "I can take it out of the frame."

"Well, do," said the woman. "Then I can fasten it to the line."

Eddie had to work hard to get the nails out, but he finally succeeded. He handed the painting to Anna Patricia and they watched as Laddie Boy was hung on the clothesline. Eddie stood the frame on the ground. It was leaning against his leg. A woman came by and said, "Little boy, put that frame over against the wall. Somebody will trip over it there beside your leg."

Eddie obediently walked over to the wall and placed the picture of the King of the Jungle against it. Then he came back to Anna Patricia, who seemed unable to take her eyes off of Laddie Boy. While they both stood there, a man came along with a box of little stickers. Each sticker had a number printed on it. Anna Patricia and Eddie watched while he stuck number eighteen on Laddie Boy. Then he hurried along from picture to picture, giving each one a number.

"Come on, Annie Pat," said Eddie. "Let's see if there are any other pictures of dogs." Anna Patricia tore her eyes away from Laddie Boy and followed Eddie. They walked around looking at all of the pictures hanging on the clothesline. More and more people were arriving. Eddie pointed to a drawing of a Welsh Terrier and said, "That's a good picture."

"Oh, it doesn't have any bright color," said Anna Patricia. "I don't think my art teacher would like that." Farther along they came to a painting of a beagle hound. "I didn't know so many people painted dogs," said Anna Patricia.

"Do you see that sticker on it?" Eddie asked. "It says *Sold*. Somebody bought it."

Soon the children were back in front of Laddie Boy. Two women were looking at it. They were laughing very hard. Anna Patricia heard one of the women say, "Who ever allowed that terrible orange dog to be hung up?"

"Isn't it awful?" said the other. The women moved along and Anna Patricia heard one say, "I see the drawing we like of the Welsh Terrier has just been given the prize."

Eddie saw Anna Patricia's face grow very pink and he could feel his ears getting hot. He knew they had turned red. He saw Anna Patricia blink her eyes to keep back the tears. Then suddenly Eddie heard voices that seemed to be quarreling. He looked to see where the voices were coming from and he saw a man holding up the picture of the King of the Jungle. He heard the man say, "This is the best thing in the show. Most of these paintings are junk. This is a very fine wood engraving and I want to buy it. I like the frame too. It's battered up, but I can fix it."

The other man was the man with the labels. Eddie heard him say, "But you don't understand. This isn't in the show. I don't know where it came from. I don't know who it belongs to, so I can't sell it to you."

By this time Eddie had pushed his way between the two tall men. He looked up and said, "It's mine."

The man who had the picture in his hands looked down at Eddie and said, "How much do you want for it?"

"Why—why—" Eddie stammered. "I don't know."

The man with the labels looked at the other man and said, "What do you think it's worth?"

"I'll give five dollars for the picture and five dollars for the frame."

"Okay?" said the label man, looking down at Eddie.

"Okay!" Eddie replied.

"Sold!" said the man with the labels. "Give the boy ten dollars."

Eddie watched the man take out his wallet and pull a ten-dollar bill out of it. He could hardly believe that he was going to receive that ten-dollar bill. After the man gave it to him, Eddie stood looking at the bill. He turned it over and looked at the other side.

Anna Patricia had come up and had watched Eddie receive the ten dollars. Eddie's grin spread all across his face as he put the bill into his pocket.

"Eddie," said Anna Patricia, "you're right! You do have valuable property. It's fabulous!"

"I can hardly wait to tell my family," said Eddie.

Anna Patricia looked very sad. "I'm going to take my painting home," she said.

"Why are you going to take it home?" Eddie asked in surprise.

"Because!" was Anna Patricia's reply, and there was a sob in her voice. "It belongs to my Aunt Mabel and I can't sell it."

"But it looks good hanging there, Annie Pat," said Eddie. "And somebody will see it and want you to paint their dog."

"No, they won't," said Anna Patricia. "They just make fun of it. I heard them." Then Anna Patricia burst into tears. "It isn't fabulous at all," she sobbed.

Eddie looked at Anna Patricia crying. Her face was so red and so wet with tears. He didn't know what to do, but he knew that when he was unhappy he always felt better if he ate something, so he said, "Oh, come on, Annie Pat. Let's go to the drugstore. I'll buy you a chocolate ice cream soda."

"Thanks," said Anna Patricia. She blew her nose and said, "I'll go get the painting of Laddie Boy. I'm going to take it home."

Eddie waited for Anna Patricia. When she came back she had the painting under her arm.

"Come on," said Eddie, "let's get the sodas."

Chapter Eight

AN UNEXPECTED CALLER

WHEN Eddie and Anna Patricia got back to the Wallaces' garage, Anna Patricia's mother was just getting out of the car. "I didn't get the prize, Mother," said Anna Patricia, and tears came into her eyes again. "I brought my painting back."

"Oh, darling, I know how disappointed you are,"

said her mother, "but you see, this exhibition is not just of paintings made by children. Many of the paintings were done by grown-ups who have been painting for a long time. You are just a little girl, and you have been painting a very short time."

"But Mother," Anna Patricia gulped. "They made fun of my painting of Laddie Boy. I heard them making fun of it. They said it was awful, didn't they, Eddie?"

"Well, I think it's good," said Eddie. "I saw a lot of their paintings that I thought were awful. I heard the man who bought my picture of the King of the Jungle say that most of the other paintings were junk."

Mrs. Wallace opened her eyes in surprise and said, "Eddie! Do you mean you sold a picture?"

"He sold it for ten dollars," said Anna Patricia.

"Eddie sold a picture for ten dollars!" her mother exclaimed. "Is Eddie painting pictures, too?"

"Oh, no," Anna Patricia replied. "It was his junk. I mean his valuable property."

Mrs. Wallace laughed. "Eddie," she said, "I never knew such a boy!"

Eddie grinned.

Anna Patricia didn't laugh, for she was still feeling bad. "I think it was mean of them to say my painting of Laddie Boy was awful," she said.

"But they didn't know that a little girl had painted it," said her mother. "If they had, I'm sure they wouldn't have made fun of your painting. For a little girl, you do very well. Very well indeed," said her mother, putting her arm around Anna Patricia.

"But it isn't fabulous, is it, Mother?" said Anna Patricia.

"It all depends what that word means to you," said her mother. "If you mean it's exciting to paint and to see a painting grow, you can call it fabulous, but if I were you, I wouldn't tell anyone that you think the painting is fabulous. I would wait and let them say it."

"I don't think anyone will ever say it," said Anna Patricia, shaking her head.

"Sure they will," said Eddie. "I guess I'll be going now," he added. "I want to tell my mother about getting this ten dollars for the King of the Jungle. Boy! Will she be surprised!"

As Eddie picked up his bicycle, Anna Patricia said, "You'll go with me to Mrs. Adams' house, won't you, Eddie? I have to finish the painting of Duchess. The end of next week we're going to the seashore for the rest of the summer."

"Oh, sure," said Eddie. "I'll be back soon. So long for now!"

As Eddie rode away, Anna Patricia said to her mother, "Eddie bought me a chocolate ice cream soda. He bought it for me 'cause I felt so bad about not getting the prize."

"That's like Eddie," said her mother. "Eddie's always ready to help. His name should be Ever-ready Eddie."

This made Anna Patricia laugh and she forgot how unhappy she had been.

The next time Eddie came over to Anna Patricia's he said, "How about going over to get Duchess so that you can finish the painting?"

"Okay," said Anna Patricia. "We'll have to walk because we have to walk Duchess back here. Oh, I do hope she won't slip her collar again."

"I'll really hold onto that dog this time," said Eddie.

When the children reached Mrs. Adams' house, Mrs. Adams came to the door in answer to Eddie's ring. "Well!" said Mrs. Adams. "Here are Eddie and Anna Patricia. Come in."

"We've come to get Duchess," said Eddie. "So Annie Pat can finish the painting."

"You can't take her today," said Mrs. Adams. "Duchess has her puppies now."

"Oh! Can we see them?" Eddie asked.

"Yes, indeed," Mrs. Adams replied. "They are in the laundry." Anna Patricia and Eddie followed Mrs. Adams to the back of the house. She led them into the laundry where she had made a bed for Duchess and her puppies. Eddie and Anna Patricia looked down at them. "Oh, aren't they the dearest little things," said Anna Patricia.

"What are you going to do with them?" Eddie asked.

"We have several friends who want one," replied Mrs. Adams.

"Are you going to sell them?" Anna Patricia asked.

"We think we'll sell two and give the others to our friends," Mrs. Adams answered. She held up one of the puppies so Eddie and Anna Patricia could look at it more closely.

"Oh, I do wish I could buy one," said Eddie. "I have ten dollars, but I guess they cost more than ten dollars."

"I wish I could, too," said Anna Patricia. "I'd love to have a puppy."

"Do they cost a lot?" Eddie asked.

"I think we'll get fifty dollars for them," said Mrs. Adams.

"For one?" Eddie asked.

"That's right," said Mrs. Adams.

"Oh," said Eddie. "Ten dollars wouldn't even buy a half a puppy."

"No," said Anna Patricia. "I guess we won't get puppies." Anna Patricia touched the soft puppy. "Even if I had won that twenty-five dollar prize, I couldn't have bought one. I could never earn that much money painting dogs."

"Even if I sold all of my valuable property, I couldn't make fifty dollars," said Eddie.

"I guess we couldn't even buy one if we put all of our money together, Eddie," said Anna Patricia.

"No," replied Eddie, "and anyway, I don't think I would like to own just half a dog."

"Well, half a dog would be better than no dog," said Anna Patricia.

"But when I patted it, I wouldn't know whether

I was patting your half or my half," said Eddie. "I wouldn't want to own half a dog."

"I'll tell you what I'll do," said Mrs. Adams. "I'll reduce the price to twenty-five dollars apiece, and I'll keep two of these puppies until the end of the summer. If you each have twenty-five dollars by September, you can each buy a puppy."

"Oh! That's wonderful!" said Eddie.

"Yes!" Anna Patricia agreed. "Maybe when I come back from the seashore I'll have twenty-five dollars. I don't know, but maybe I could earn twenty-five dollars."

"Not painting dogs, you won't," said Eddie.

"I could reduce the price," said Anna Patricia. "Mrs. Adams reduced her price from fifty dollars to twenty-five dollars. I'm going to reduce my price from fifty cents to twenty-five cents."

"Annie Pat! At that price, do you know how many dogs you'd have to paint to earn twenty-five dollars?" said Eddie.

"How many?" Anna Patricia asked.

"I'll have to find out with a pencil and paper," replied Eddie, looking around. Mrs. Adams handed Eddie a pencil and a piece of paper. "Now let's see," said Eddie. He wet the lead pencil and wrote down, *Twenty-five dogs.* "No," he said, "I mean twenty-five cents. No! I guess I mean twenty-five dollars."

"That's right," said Anna Patricia, leaning over the paper. "Now divide twenty-five dollars by twenty-five dogs."

"Annie Pat!" Eddie cried. "Don't mix me up. You can't divide dollars with dogs. Anybody knows that."

"No, of course not," said Anna Patricia. "It's the other way around. You have to divide the dogs with the dollars."

"Now you keep out of this, Annie Pat," said Eddie. "I can do this by myself." Eddie put down some figures on the paper, but before he could go any further, Anna Patricia said, "Eddie! I would have to paint one hundred dogs!"

Eddie looked up. "How do you know?" he asked.

"I did it in my head," said Anna Patricia. "I just moved the decimal point. First I moved it from before the two to behind the two and I knew that was ten dogs. Then I moved it behind the five and I knew that was a hundred dogs."

"It would be more than that," said Eddie, " 'cause I get twenty-two cents for holding the dogs, and if you reduce the price to twenty-five cents, you will only get three cents a dog."

"Three cents!" exclaimed Anna Patricia. "Eddie! I couldn't pay you twenty-two cents if I only got twenty-five cents. I would pay you ten cents."

Eddie did a little mental arithmetic himself and said, "Eleven cents! Then you would get fourteen cents. So you would have to paint—let me see."

"Oh, don't see," said Anna Patricia. "I don't want to see that many dogs. It's too many dogs!"

Mrs. Adams sat on a chair, listening to Eddie and Anna Patricia. "Yes," she said. "That is indeed a lot of dogs."

"You will keep the two puppies, though, won't you, Mrs. Adams?" said Anna Patricia.

"I promise you, I'll keep them," said Mrs. Adams.

"When I come back from the seashore, I'll finish the painting of Duchess," said Anna Patricia. "And

if you like it, it will only cost twenty-five cents."

"Oh, I'm sure I'll like it," said Mrs. Adams.

The children said good-bye to Mrs. Adams, and both of them went home.

Several days later, Anna Patricia and Eddie were in the Wallaces' garage. Anna Patricia's mother had asked them to straighten up the part of the garage that Anna Patricia called her studio. The big overhead door was shut, but the little door was open. Anna Patricia was holding the dustpan and Eddie was busy sweeping some litter into it when a shadow fell on the floor nearby. Eddie looked up. To his great surprise, there was a dog. A young poodle, not much more than a puppy, had just walked in the door. "Well! Look at that!" Eddie exclaimed.

"It's a poodle!" cried Anna Patricia.

Eddie stood with the brush in his hand and Anna Patricia held the dustpan, looking at the unexpected visitor. "Maybe he came to have his picture painted," said Anna Patricia. Eddie and Anna Patricia both laughed over this.

The dog walked around the garage, smelling here

and there. Finally the dog came to Eddie. He looked up at Eddie and gave a sharp bark. "Who are you?" said Eddie. "Did you come to have your picture painted?" Eddie leaned down and patted the dog. Then he noticed that the dog was without a collar. "Annie Pat!" he cried. "This dog doesn't have any collar on. He must be lost."

Anna Patricia looked down at the dog. Her forehead was wrinkled. "What shall we do with him?" she asked.

"We can't just let him run off," said Eddie. "You know those dogcatchers. They'll grab him if they see him. You remember what happened to Duchess!"

"Well, he can't stay here," said Anna Patricia, "because we're going away."

"I'll take him home with me," said Eddie. "He's a nice dog and I never had a poodle before."

"Well, if you find out who he belongs to, be sure to ask them if they want his picture painted," said Anna Patricia.

"Oh, sure," Eddie replied. Eddie picked up the dog and said, "I'll just put him in the basket on my bike and ride him over to our house."

The dog was quite happy to ride in the basket. When Eddie reached home he lifted the dog out of the basket and carried him into the house. Eddie called out, "Mother! Hi, Mother! I've brought a lost dog home! He's a nice poodle. He's just a pup."

Mrs. Wilson came to look at the dog. Eddie looked up at his mother and said, "Somebody has to take care of him, don't they? He can't just run the streets, can he?"

"I guess not," said his mother.

"Oh, that's great!" said Eddie. "I knew you would want me to take care of him, Mother."

"You must try to find the owner, Eddie," said his mother. "Go telephone to the police and tell them you have found a white poodle who isn't wearing a collar."

Eddie's face grew long. "Right away?" he cried. "Can't I wait a while?"

"No," replied his mother. "You must do it at once. The owner is probably worried about the dog."

Eddie went to the telephone and dialed the police station. When Eddie hung up the telephone a few minutes later, his face was very bright. "They haven't heard from anybody about a lost dog," he said. "Now I'd better go to the store and buy some dog food."

"You'll have to spend your own money," said his mother.

"Okay," said Eddie. "Don't let him out while I'm away."

"Very well," his mother replied, "but hurry back and give this dog a bath. He must have spent the night in a coal yard. You had better clean him up before your father sees him. You know he's not too fond of lost dogs, even when they're clean."

Eddie hurried out and he hurried back. He fed the dog and he washed him. Eddie was delighted to have a dog in the house once more.

Eddie's brothers and even his father liked the poodle, but his mother said Eddie should watch the daily paper to see if anyone listed a lost dog. Eddie didn't watch very carefully so his mother had to do the watching. A week passed but no advertisement appeared.

Before Anna Patricia left for the seashore, she telephoned to Eddie to say good-bye. "Do you still have the poodle?" she asked.

"I still have him," Eddie replied. "He's a swell dog. I'll see you when you get back. Have fun while you're away!"

The week after Anna Patricia departed, Mrs. Wilson was reading the local paper. "Eddie!" she called. Eddie came downstairs, followed by the dog. When he saw his mother with the paper in her hand he knew at once what his mother was going to tell him. "Is it about the dog?" he said.

"I think so," his mother replied. She read the description of the dog to Eddie. Then at the end she read, "Reward, five dollars."

"I guess that's him," said Eddie. Eddie patted the dog. "I'll miss him," he said. "He's such a swell dog."

That afternoon Eddie returned the dog to its owner, who was delighted to have him back. She had been away from home, she told Eddie, and didn't know that the dog had run away from the friend who was supposed to take care of him. When Eddie came home with the five-dollar bill he had received as a reward, he said to his mother, "Isn't that wonderful, Mother? Now I have five dollars more toward the German shepherd."

"German shepherd!" said his mother. "What German shepherd?"

"The puppy Mrs. Adams is saving for me," Eddie replied. "She's going to let me have it for only twenty-five dollars. Isn't that great?"

"Well," said his mother. She paused a moment, then she said, "After all, only a dog can eat up that dog food that you bought for the poodle, so maybe you're right."

Chapter Nine

BACK TO SCHOOL

WHILE Anna Patricia was away at the seashore, Eddie went around the neighborhood with Boodles while Boodles took photographs of cats. Sometimes the cats kept perfectly still, but when they would not, Eddie was delighted to hold them. He was only scratched once.

Eddie was surprised to see how many pictures Boodles was able to sell. He soon saw that Boodles was a very good photographer. Boodles always gave Eddie his two cents, and by the end of the summer Eddie's pocket jingled with pennies.

When a newspaper contest for photographs was announced over the radio, Eddie told Boodles about it. "You should send some of your pictures in to the contest," said Eddie. "Maybe you would win a prize." Boodles thought it was a fine idea, so he mailed some of his best prints to the newspaper and waited to see whether he would receive a prize.

The very day the prize-winning photographs were published, Anna Patricia was dusting the living room for her mother. She picked up the newspaper to put it on the table beside her father's chair. As she placed it on the table, her eye fell on a photograph that was printed on the front page. Above the photograph were the words, "Prize-winning photographs submitted by local boy." Anna Patricia looked at the picture. It was a photograph of a boy with his arms around a dog. She looked more closely, and to her amazement she saw that it was a photograph of Eddie holding an Airedale. The dog was licking Eddie's cheek. Anna Patricia then read the words under the picture. "Boswell Cary won the prize in the six-to-eleven age group with this photograph of his friend, Edward Wilson, another local boy, and a dog named Brownie."

Boswell Cary, Anna Patricia thought. "Why, that's Boodles!" she cried. Anna Patricia dropped the paper and went to the telephone. She dialed the Wilsons' number and listened to the ringing.

Eddie picked up the receiver. "Hello," he said.

"Is that you, Eddie?" said Anna Patricia.

"Hi, Annie Pat!" said Eddie. "When did you get back?"

"Edward Wilson!" Anna Patricia exclaimed. "You've been dog holding for Boodles! I saw your picture in the paper. You promised me you would not hold dogs for Boodles. You said you would only hold cats for him. You said he promised not to take any pictures of dogs and *he did!* I saw it in the paper."

"Well, I only did it once for him," said Eddie. "I only did it that once when I held Brownie. I don't know what you're so mad about. I held Brownie for you, didn't I?"

"Yes. But when you held Brownie for me he didn't win a prize," Anna Patricia retorted.

"That was your Aunt Mabel's cocker spaniel that didn't win the prize," said Eddie. "What's the matter with you, Annie Pat? Aren't you glad Boodles won the prize?"

"Well, I don't care," said Anna Patricia. "He should have won it with cats because dogs around here belong to me. I paint the dogs, and you are dog holder for me and cat holder for Boodles."

"Now, Annie Pat," said Eddie. "I had to hold that dog for Boodles. Mrs. Brownley asked me to do it. And anyway, didn't I get Mrs. Brownley to let you paint Brownie?"

"Yes," said Anna Patricia, sounding as though her fire had burned out.

"Well, then," said Eddie, "what have you got to be mad about?"

"What was the prize Boodles won?" Anna Patricia asked.

"Five dollars," Eddie replied.

"Five dollars!" Anna Patricia exclaimed. "Everybody gets money but me! You got ten dollars for your junk—"

"Valuable property," said Eddie.

"And Boodles gets five dollars for his photograph," Anna Patricia finished her sentence.

"I haven't got enough money to buy that puppy yet," said Eddie.

"I'll never have enough," said Anna Patricia, in a discouraged tone of voice.

"You all fixed up to go back to school?" Eddie asked, changing the subject.

"Oh, I have a new pencil box," said Anna Patricia.

"I have a whole dozen pencils with my name on them in gold letters," said Eddie.

"Well, I'll see you in school next Monday," said Anna Patricia.

"So long," said Eddie, as he hung up the telephone.

On Monday morning, when Eddie arrived at school, he was glad to see all of his friends after the long vacation. He told Anna Patricia about finding the owner of the poodle. "I got a reward," said Eddie. "Five dollars."

"Oh, Eddie," said Anna Patricia, "now you have fifteen dollars, haven't you?"

"That's right," said Eddie, "but I need ten dollars more before I can get that German shepherd."

"Do you think Mrs. Adams still has those puppies she promised to keep for us?" Anna Patricia asked.

"I guess so," Eddie replied. "She said she would keep them until September."

"It's September now," said Anna Patricia, "and I don't have twenty-five dollars. I have to work hard painting dogs, while you can just sell your junk."

"Valuable property, Annie Pat," said Eddie.

The new fourth grade teacher called the class to order. Eddie looked at her. She had red hair and blue eyes. Her name was Miss Scattergood, which he thought was a very nice name. The first thing Miss Scattergood did after she called the roll was to ask the children to tell what they had done during their vacation. Of course, Boodles told about taking photographs and winning the prize in the newspaper contest. Anna Patricia told how she had painted pictures of dogs. The children made sounds that showed that they thought painting dogs was quite wonderful. Eddie told of how he had held the dogs for Anna Patricia and the cats for Boodles. He also told about the day Mrs. Brownley's bird, Pippa, got out of its cage and how it got back again.

Some of the boys in the class had made things out of wood, bookends and racks. Many of the girls had made doll dresses and paper dolls. One girl, Margie, had learned to knit. She had made a scarf that she could wear in the winter.

When they had all told of their summer activities, Miss Scattergood said, "Don't you think it would be a good idea if you all brought the things you made to school? Then we could have an exhibition."

"Oh, yes!" the children agreed.

"I don't have anything to show," said Eddie. "I just helped Annie Pat and Boodles."

"Didn't you make anything, Eddie?" Miss Scattergood asked.

"I made ten dollars when I sold a picture that I had in my valuable property," said Eddie.

"What do you mean, your valuable property?" Miss Scattergood asked.

All the children in the room knew what Eddie meant and they all called out, "He means his junk!"

Miss Scattergood laughed. "Well, if Eddie can sell anything out of it for ten dollars, it can't be junk," she said. "It must be valuable property."

Eddie knew then and there that he was going to like Miss Scattergood. He could imagine her scattering good everywhere she went, like Santa Claus.

"When shall we bring our things?" Anna Patricia asked.

"Bring them next Monday," Miss Scattergood replied.

On Monday morning, Anna Patricia arrived at school with three paintings under her arm. She had brought the painting of Aunt Mabel's cocker spaniel and the one that belonged to her cousin. She also brought Aunt Mabel's cat. When Boodles saw the painting of the cat, he said, "I don't think you should put that cat picture in the exhibition."

"But my Aunt Mabel likes it very much," said Anna Patricia, "and anyway, you put your dog picture in."

By the time all of the children arrived, there were many things for the exhibition. Some of the children had been working on pottery. There were ashtrays and bowls and even rabbits. Several of the boys had worked in wood, and besides bookends and shelves there were some strange-looking animals carved out of wood. Girls who had been sewing brought beanbags and pot holders that they had made. Sidney had worked on a picture book over the summer. She had pasted old Christmas cards into a book. There were Boodles' photographs and Margie's knitted scarf.

"Is there going to be a prize?" Margie asked the teacher.

"Not exactly," Miss Scattergood replied, "but there will be awards. A three-star award, a two-star award, and a one-star award."

"Who is going to choose what gets the awards?" Eddie asked.

"We're going to have a jury," Miss Scattergood answered.

"What's a jury?" Boodles asked.

"A jury is made up of several persons," said Miss Scattergood. "They will look at all of the things you have brought and they will decide about the stars."

"Who's on the jury?" Sidney asked.

"We're going to have one child from the third, the fourth, the fifth, and the sixth grades," Miss Scattergood answered, "and of course, Mr. Taylor, the principal, and myself."

"Where's the show going to be?" asked Eddie.

"In the first floor corridor, right beside the front door," said Miss Scattergood. "If everything you have brought has a tag on it with your name, we can take your things downstairs now."

The whole class followed Miss Scattergood downstairs and into the corridor. They stood and watched while the children who had brought things for the exhibition placed them on a large table. Boodles

tacked his photographs on the wall and Anna Patricia fastened her paintings to the wall with push-pins.

At lunchtime the jury held its meeting and it didn't take them long to agree about the awards.

Anna Patricia could hardly eat her lunch, she was so anxious to see what would be awarded the three stars. As soon as she finished her lunch she ran up the steps to the first floor corridor. She looked at her paintings, and there stuck on the painting of Aunt Mabel's marmalade cat were three gold stars.

Anna Patricia stood in front of her painting, admiring the three gold stars. Some big girls from the sixth grade stopped to look at the paintings and Anna Patricia heard one of the girls say, "I think those paintings are wonderful! Just think, Anna Patricia Wallace did them. I don't know her, but she certainly is a good artist."

"And she's only in the fourth grade," said another girl.

"I could never do anything like that," said the third girl. "I think it's fabulous!" Anna Patricia walked away feeling tingly right down into her toes.

Boodles was pleased when he discovered that his photographs had received the two-star award, and Margie got the one-star for her knitted scarf.

It wasn't until several days later that Eddie had an opportunity to talk to Mr. Kilpatrick, for the policeman had been very busy with the new children. One afternoon Mr. Kilpatrick was standing alone on the corner when Eddie came along. "Hello, Mr. Kilpatrick," said Eddie.

"Hello, Eddie," Mr. Kilpatrick replied, "and how did you and Anna Patricia get along with the dog painting business?"

"Oh, it was great!" said Eddie. "You know, Mr. Kilpatrick, sometimes things aren't the way you think they're going to be because they get sort of mixed around. Like Boodles and Annie Pat's prizes."

"How was that?" Mr. Kilpatrick asked.

"Well. You know, I was dog holder for Annie Pat and I was cat holder for Boodles. But do you know what? Boodles got a prize for his picture of a dog and Annie Pat got a prize for her painting of a cat. You see what I mean, Mr. Kilpatrick?"

"I do indeed!" said Mr. Kilpatrick. "It's this mixing business that makes everything so interesting."

Just then, Anna Patricia dashed up. "Oh, Eddie!" she cried. "My daddy is going to buy the German shepherd puppy for me because I got the three stars."

"That's wonderful, Annie Pat," said Eddie. "I only need ten dollars more and I can get mine. Mrs. Adams said she would hold it a little longer."

"You'll get it, Eddie," said Mr. Kilpatrick, "sure as my name's Kilpatrick. I know you'll get that puppy—but I hope you won't start holding somebody's snakes in order to earn the ten dollars."

About the Author

Carolyn Haywood is distinguished both as author and illustrator of children's books. Her first book was published in 1939. Since then she has had twenty-six books published and has become one of the most widely read American writers for younger children.

Carolyn Haywood was born in Philadelphia and still lives in that city. She is a graduate of the Philadelphia Normal School and studied at the Pennsylvania Academy of Fine Arts, where she won the Cresson European Scholarship for distinguished work. Miss Haywood calls herself a "grand-pupil" of the great American illustrator, Howard Pyle, having studied with three of his distinguished pupils, Elizabeth Shippen Elliott, Violet Oakley, and Jessie Willcox Smith. She is also a portrait painter and has specialized in portraits of children. Her experience in this field has given her a sympathetic understanding of children and their interests, which has made her peculiarly well fitted to write and illustrate for them. She is continuing her portrait work with commissions in New York, Philadelphia, and other eastern cities.